TOMORROW'S
END

J.M. CLARK

Tomorrow's End
by J.M. Clark

Copyright © 2018 J.M. Clark
All Rights Reserved

Cover art by Panagiotis Lampridis
Edited by https://espressoeditor.com/
Formatted by FastFormatting@gmail.com

Fraternity Rose Publishing

FRATERNITY ROSE
PUBLISHING

Join the mailing list and receive free giveaways and exclusive content:

Website: http://www.writtenbyjmclark.com
Email: writtenbyjmclark@gmail.com

PART I

AWAKENING

1

BRANDEN

DOING ANYTHING, NO MATTER HOW GOOD OR BAD, THAT THING COULD eventually become second nature. "Easy as pie," his mother would say when explaining something to him she thought to be simple. "Easy as pie" or "Easy peasy," she would shout and slap him on the shoulder or mess up his hair. He missed the goofy way she had about her.

Her lighthearted teasing taught him all behaviors were learned, and even something so vile as killing could become a skill. Especially if you thought you had a good reason to be doing the killing. Having a reason to do something breeds repetition, and repetition breeds skill. He knew this to be true, and the young man had his reasons. He'd become very skilled at the work of—taking life.

Brandon sat in the front seat of the van he'd procured earlier from a group of men. At least, he thought they were men, but deep inside, he knew he could be wrong; nothing was as it seemed. His time out in the world taught him this long ago. His parents had theories on exactly who the men driving the vans were. He'd always thought of them as hunters, but they were not; they were lazy bullies, driving around teaming up on good people, killing and taking. They'd tried to take him one day. They'd failed. He was different though, and what he did was definitely hunting. His mother taught him how to hunt, and good for him, to have had her in his life, to have had a parent sufficient with the skill of hunting in this new world. This was the reason why he'd not been taken away to wherever it was they took those they happened to stumble upon while doing their sweeps. Again, what they did was not hunting.

For Branden, it didn't matter who or what they were. They now lay dead in the third-row seat of their own van. Today's kill was fresh, so there was no fear of rotting…just yet. He'd take care of the bodies long before they could go bad. *Too late, they are already bad guys.* He smirked at the thought of something his father would say if he'd been in the situation himself.

The young man struck a match as he balanced a cigarette between his lips, the same way he'd seen his father do a thousand times before. He rolled down the window of the van by pushing in a small button to his left. Operating the vehicles were once an annoyance. It took him a full weekend to learn how to drive one of the hulking machines named cars. They covered ground faster than any man could walk, and he'd grown tired of walking long ago. Now though, it was easy as pie.

Cupping his free hand over the hand holding the cigarette, he lit it aflame. Of course, there was no reason to cover the cigarette when lighting it, but the motion was something else he'd seen his father do, so he did it as well. Made him feel older than he was.

He let out small puffs of smoke into the car as he flicked the match out into the grass. He liked the way the smoke smelled; it reminded him of the basement in virtually every home his family had lived in. His mother always ordered his father to either smoke outside or in the basement. Nostalgia was the cure for not forgetting important memories, the kind with intense meaning. Whether you realized it in the moment or not—the sensation of experiencing memories you once thought forgotten were alone worth the risk of lung cancer. If his mother were alive, she would slap the back of his head at the thought of him smoking cigarettes.

He wondered what she would think about his new hobby of choice. Killing was a far cry from shooting baskets in the backyard of some long-forgotten family's home. Times and expectations change though, and people change, sometimes by force. The type of change occurring by force usually ended up being something one could not come back from.

He took another drag from the cigarette and looked into the rearview mirror at the two bodies crumpled into a heap of limbs, their dead stares reflecting whatever it was men saw just before leaving the current plane of existence. Had to be something calming, he thought, because their eyes seemed at peace. Good for them, he concluded with a weak nod of his head.

The men didn't appear to be in a rush to go anywhere anytime soon. He took another puff of the cigarette and directed his attention back to the light show he'd been watching for the last hour or so. He thought maybe he was watching the end of the world...but that had already happened long ago, so it had to be something different.

He then wondered if he should be afraid of what was happening about a mile away. You know, what if some of the burning shrapnel happened to make it to where he was and crushed him. He doubted it, but it could happen. There was quite a lot going on up there.

From his current perch on a hill somewhere in Indiana, Branden prepared yet another mass exodus from the planet. He'd known he was in Indiana because he noticed all of the worn-out signs as he stalked the two gentlemen in the back of the van throughout the state. He was not afraid though; the bottom line was death, and he had no qualms with meeting that particular fate. "Death was eventual for all lucky enough to experience life." Another saying of his mother's, who had been a teacher in the Old World before everything had changed. She most definitely never stopped using her passion for teaching and gaining knowledge, even though he became her only pupil. He was thankful.

He ashed the cigarette into the tray just beneath the dashboard of the van. He'd never seen fire rain down from the sky. It was hard to believe what he was seeing. Burning objects fell from something that could have been a flying small town in the sky. So many falling pieces chipping away and cascading to the ground.

The sound coming from the thing, or in the same direction, was soothing. He'd never heard anything like it. It resembled a horn, a very loud horn...but there was also pain in what he was hearing. It was strange to him, but the large object rapidly losing pieces of itself almost seemed to be screaming. The more pieces it lost, the more the horns sounded and the harsher they became.

The cigarette dwindled down to the butt while he watched the show out the windshield of the stolen van. He reached outside the window to mash out the remaining embers on the side of the van. Turning around in his seat, he calmly spoke to the bodies in the back. "What the hell do you figure is going on out there, guys?" They didn't respond.

He then glanced up to the badges hanging from the rearview mirror and grabbed them, reading the names to himself. "I'm sorry, Mark, and Clayton...forgive me—what do you think is going on way out there?" His eyes surveyed the bodies; they'd begun to attract flies, and he rolled the window back up. "Yeah, I don't know either."

Again, his attention moved back to the raining fire. He began tapping on the steering wheel with his thumbs, pondering what could be going on and if it was smart to get a closer look. The van would likely draw too much attention if he chose to drive into the area. It was far off, so he didn't know if there was fighting going on, but common sense told him something had damaged the thing falling from the sky in scattered fragments. He made up his mind and opened the driver side door to step out into the grass.

He closed the door behind him. Walking toward the back of the van, he felt a surge of pain attack his brain. At least that's what it felt like to him. The horn sound became louder, causing him to turn around and look at the object floating in the sky just in time to see the thing split in two. It was enormous. When the split occurred, he thought he would be able to see some of the inner workings of the object, even from this distance, but he could not. It was totally empty from what he could see. He wanted to get a better look, so he staggered a few steps closer to the front of the van.

The sound suddenly became so loud and disturbing it broke him down to one knee as he brought both hands to his ears and closed his eyes. The noise was deafening as he leaned against the side of the van. The young man opened his eyes, his pupils promptly darting up to watch both monstrous pieces of the object fall from the sky in a grand opera of death and downfall. It was an extravagant show lasting longer than expected, but not nearly long enough to appease his curiosity. He needed to know more.

While the halves were falling, there were smaller flying objects moving quickly around them, shooting blue beams at each colossal piece. He thought maybe those tiny flying gadgets were the cause of the damage. *What else could bring such destruction to a monstrosity so formidable? What exactly is it?* His brain was popping with questions he could not possibly answer on his own.

A spaceship, he supposed, but could it be a real thing? Of course not; it could be domestic though. Had to be domestic, right? His father told him that the government, prior to the sickness, was involved in some dark development types of ideas. It was a possibility.

After the worst of the sounds quieted, he was able to make it back to his feet. He slapped dirt and rocks off his knee, setting his attention back to the matter at hand. The falling spaceship business wasn't going anywhere, and he had business of his own to take care of.

After making his way to the back of the van, he peered through the back window while pulling on the latch to open the two doors of the trunk. The crumpled bodies could be seen in the seat just behind the trunk. They didn't look real to him by the way they were folded up and around each other.

He found out quickly in his new line of work, the decomposing process named rigor mortis did not set in for a little while after death, still leaving time to fold bodies in hiding places without too much strife in dealing with the stiffening of arms and legs. He smiled at the balled-up men, grabbed a red plastic container, and closed both back doors before moving to the right side of the van to open the sliding door, giving him access to the first row of seats. Stepping into the van, he reached into the passenger seat to grab his backpack, which he tossed outside. He twisted off the cap of the container and doused the

7

dead men and everything else in the van with the contents of the red container.

After finishing off the container and tossing it down the hill the van was parked on, he walked around to the front and sat on the hood. Branden, who now regarded himself as a hunter of men, removed a pack of Marlboro Reds from the pocket of his dirty jeans. He wiped the gasoline on his hands onto the blue blood-stained NY Giants tee shirt that once belonged to his father. The shirt, along with the backpack of other shirts and another pair of jeans were all he took from his old home.

After his first killing—the killing of the men responsible for taking his parents away from him when they were doing nothing more than trying to survive in a world guilty of forgetting about them—he returned to the home he and his family were staying in before the white van came. He knew he needed to bury the bodies, but he also returned because he had no idea where else to go. He was but a lost child, crying, struggling to not heave up his guts, and wanting his parents.

This was before killing became a skill to him. The finely tuned weapon he'd made himself into over time would never be so weak... ever again. The thought of being so distraught for simply taking the lives of the men evil enough to steal everything from him was enough to conjure up shame right then and there.

He often tried not to think about his former self. Wasting his days running around an abandoned neighborhood, shooting countless shots at a basketball hoop on the property of someone buried within their cellar while he was dressed in the same clothes they had died in. He should have been more focused; he could have been guarding his home—maybe he could have saved them. He had to wear that until the day he died.

Luckily, he was able to gut the bastards with one of their own knives in the van before they were too far from his house, or else he'd have been lost when trying to find his way back. That had been a different van of course, not the one he sat on today, smoking and watching the smaller floating objects moving back and forth with nothing to shoot their blue beams of light at.

The days in the beginning were filled with hunting, driving a white van, killing some more, then hiding the van before taking another one. Couldn't leave evidence to what he'd been up to. He knew they were looking for him, but he didn't mind one bit. His prey had no chance in searching for what was hunting it down. To keep hunting or to take a brief detour—that was the question he reflected upon.

"Fuck it," he said aloud and jumped down from the van. He grabbed his backpack, slung it over his shoulder, and walked to the passenger side window. He took one more long pull on the cigarette, blowing the smoke into the air and taking in the smell and the comfort that came along with the aroma. He shut his eyes and inhaled deeply. *I miss you, Dad,* he thought before opening his eyes. Then he tossed the half-smoked stick into the van.

He took a step back and watched it light up as bright as the horizon before him. The day was full of fire, he thought. After standing there for some time, watching the van turn into a metallic ball of fire, he started off in the direction of the area where the flying craft fell from the sky. What he hadn't decided upon was if the vessel was domestic or from…outer space. He thought himself crazy to give any real credence to the idea. The problem was, his eyes did not lie… he saw what he saw.

Branden swept the dark brown locks of hair from his eyes, slipped both arms through the backpack straps, and walked toward where the action was.

2

_____

TEACHER SIMON

WHEN ASKED DID HE WANT A ROOM ON THE SAME FLOOR AS SIRUS, BY Sirus…Teacher Simon declined and requested a room in the basement of the Palace. He preferred quiet, and while Sirus was not loud at all, the floor housing his office was for working, for completing issues the program director needed completed. Teacher Simon wanted a separation of church and state, as some would say.

He'd always been a fan of music, for as long as he could remember, and his memory stretched a millennium. Through the current reality and a billion others, he'd always had an affinity for creating music. Like his own home of Lohar, Simon wanted his room in the Palace to reflect his interest. There was no need for a bed; he did not sleep in the same way their specimens slept. His room hidden in the basement of the Palace was full of instruments. Only wind instruments though, and a harp.

There was no need for food; he did not eat. There was no need for clothing outside of the suit he wore, for he did not become dirty, nor did he sweat. There was no shower in his room for the very same reason. He required nothing more than his instruments, and over time with Sirus, this became known. They'd started the Palace Program experiment together, with Sirus as the lead. Simon was his number two, there to make sure that no heavy lifting or dirty work got in the way of the final results.

Throughout every replication of the Earth experiment, he'd played this role without failure, and comfortably, because to a certain degree, it fit his nature. Simon being the darkness after the light was of the utmost importance to both himself and Sirus. One could not exist without the other within the confines of the controlled conditions. And Simon took his job seriously.

He sat with his harp, plucking away at the strings, his long fingers gliding over the thin threads masterfully. If only those within the Palace or outside of it could hear the pain in his instrument. The pain he felt for what had happened to Sirus. He did not need to be there to know the program director was in pain, they were connected. Simon did not necessarily feel the same pain his partner felt...but the stress was shared. He felt enough to know that Sirus was not dead, for they could not die inside of the reality they created—but he could be hurt and pushed away.

The song he played came from that stress, the pain of his manifestation link being severed from the place they'd worked on together. Simon's face was a cloak of chiseled stone; there were no emotions to be read. All feeling came from the harp his fingers brought to life. With eyes lazily shut, his lips pressed together tightly, and his face aimed to the ceiling of his room, he played and played until all of his emotions were out—his feelings through music expressing exactly what Sirus being pushed away from their "thing" meant.

Over the short amount of time they'd worked together on this particular experiment, he'd gone by many different names. Simon this time around, but there were countless names, some lost to the sands of time, buried beneath the water level, never to be discovered again. For every civilization, regardless of the Earth's version, he was the yin to Sirus's yang. This was how the specimens could see one of them as the focal point. Again, one could not exist without the other—and Simon was damn good at his job.

Without the light in the world, there could only be darkness, and Simon was the darkness. His purpose was to be the one everyone pointed at as the vile, cunning stranger. Sirus played the role of the praised. So, he would play while thinking of what needed to be done. There were elements at play he and Sirus could not account for. As long as everything happened the way they intended, there would be no prying eyes stepping into what they were trying to do with their specimens. That time was long gone; Sirus had gone too far tinkering with the results and "having too much fun," as he'd heard his long-time friend say many times before.

He knew what needed to be done to finalize the reality for optimal results. Without Sirus present, simply playing the role of Teacher Simon would no longer get the job done. The "adversary" or "the roaring lion"—as he'd been labeled in the version prior to the current —would serve him best. Before the entire experiment was shut down, he would need to set matters straight in order to allow life as their specimens understood it to go on for a few thousand years more.

There was only one person created to bring the next variant of the planet around to how it was always meant to be. Sirus was confident that he'd gotten the DNA strand correct this time around.

As his fingers moved delicately but with rapid fluidity along the strings of the harp, Simon had a quick thought pertaining to rear-ranging what steps he would take to see the beginning of the new version though…

"What a shame they cannot hear my songs," he said. Probably best for them anyway; some specimens had been known to drive them-selves crazy listening to his sweet sounds. Some frequencies were of this reality, but others could not be fathomed by the human mind. One radical pluck of his harp could send a man mad or push the subject into complete servitude to him.

For the remainder of the night, what would end up being nine hours straight, he played and thought. No rest, no breaks…his fingers never tired of doing their work, and his mind never stopped figuring out possibilities and algorithms to best finish their work. The work *would* be finished though. Simon was sure of that.

3

MARY

MAYBE SHE WAS JUST A YOUNG STUPID GIRL FROM THE PALACE. A GIRL without an understanding of matters as they were in the world...the real world, just as Carla had said so many times. *How many?* she asked herself. How many lost their lives in just the last thirty minutes of what she thought could possibly be a fight? A chance to get revenge on those from elsewhere, her creators, the people responsible for killing Jacob. All of these questions permeated her mind as she fell behind Dale.

Dale grabbed her hand as they ran down a corridor leading to what would eventually be a staircase in the eastern end of the Palace, or what was left of it. The fighting still taking place as she escaped the scene was not kind to the structure of the rebel Palace. There were craters in walls where there were none only an hour ago. Chunks of caulk and plaster were scattered along the ground everywhere she looked.

She could easily outpace him in a race if she chose to, but she did not want to leave. With every step taken, she wanted to take two in the opposite direction and join the dance of life and death with those she'd ordered to fight on her behalf...How could she run away now? To show cowardice and leave the Eagle squad to die for her sake...it wasn't right. They'd put their lives in her hands, and she had squandered it all in mere minutes.

Mary wanted to pull her hand free and run back to the front of the Palace to be with them—be with them, win or die with them. The farther they ran from the battle, the fewer and fewer gunshots she heard. That meant her side dwindled in numbers and morale, and they needed her. *Die with them, the fighting is done. There is only death back there*, a voice said in her mind. It was her own voice.

Death wasn't so bad; she knew this to be true. And she had no reason to want to live. Her fate was on the killing field, and she wanted it more than she wanted to continue living. How much she wanted to continue killing scared her. Those from her own side who came to grab her and send her to safety had nearly died by her own hands. In the mindset she found herself, it was hard to tell friend from foe.

If they were lucky enough to get away through an exit in the basement of the Palace, they would be the only two left from what was a group of hundreds an hour or so ago. How fast the time passes when one is full of self-pride, not taking the strengths or weaknesses of the group into consideration. She didn't have a scratch on her body, and the thought made her grimace as they took a sharp left down another corridor. *You must earn the deaths of those who trusted you. You have barely begun...go back*, the voice said.

Mary could see Dale had been shot in his left back shoulder. The green jacket he wore had a dark purple stain where blood was oozing from the wound. She thought he needed to remove the jacket entirely and use some type of tourniquet to put pressure on the wound, but there was no time to give his injury the attention it so urgently needed. His arm hung at his side like a dead piece of meat, wriggling in the wind behind him as he ran as hard as he could in front of her, holding her hand the whole time. Everyone fighting for her was either dying or maimed, everyone but her.

"We are yours to command," were his words when they were whole. She had stared into the eyes of hundreds of men and women who'd lived through the worst experiences any being to ever draw breath could possibly imagine. The loss of their children, spouses, and friends. They had traversed a dead planet for twenty years in hopes of finding a purpose to live when there was nothing left to believe in. Their gods and governments failed them, or so they thought. Even still, they kept on pushing for a better tomorrow, only to die at the command of a careless child who had just recently came to find herself on the outside months before.

Should have just come with me, child. The voice in her mind began to sound like Sirus; it was her, but different. She thought she could hear the smile on his face. A face she'd seen change into a million different faces, a billion faces if she had to guess, all in equal pain as he writhed and flailed relentlessly on the same field Logan saw to have an impromptu meeting of the minds. He was not smiling the last time she laid eyes on him. Something told her he was not dead though. Yeah, she'd seen the ship come crumbling down, but still…she could feel him inside of her. Speaking to her.

She felt all of the Palace-born soldiers—felt connected to them—and she knew why. They were all different.

"Run faster! I have to get you out of here before they catch up to us!" Dale screamed at her without looking back. "Marcella and Kristopher won't be able to hold them off for long," he said, panting the whole time. She knew he was tired and in severe pain, even still—the only thing he could think about was getting her to safety. There was no place safe though. The Order had taken over the planet before she was even born (with Sirus's DNA). Wherever they escaped to, if they made it out, the new place would be equally unsafe. Mary was fed up with others dying and getting hurt for her sake.

It would be easier to die with them. The voice of Sirus said in her mind in a nonchalant manner. Mary pushed the voice from her head just as she and Dale burst through an exit door and began taking the steps as fast as they could.

Had it all been for nothing? she wondered. Dale held one of her hands, dragging her along, and in her other hand, she tightly gripped the dull piece of metal used to destroy the massive ship. The device now felt dead in her hand. Since she'd used the weapon there on the field as Logan lay dead, it had been utterly useless. She would not get rid of it though, she only needed to figure out how she had come to use its power. The force of the weapon was a game changer—she knew it the moment she'd seen it at work. Everyone had seen its power.

After reaching the basement, Dale released her hand to fling open the door at the bottom of the steps. He slammed the door behind them and stopped. Bending over, Dale placed his hands on his knees.

Mary watched him labor to catch his breath. She placed a hand on his back, but Dale stood up and pushed her hand away. "I'm okay, Mary. I don't need to be coddled," he said without looking at her. She'd embarrassed him. Mary didn't feel tired at all; in fact, she felt like she could fight all day if necessary, and maybe he noticed her endurance as well. This could be what had him aggravated. She'd never claimed to be an expert on the male ego, but she knew pride was heavily present within them.

"I'm sorry," she began. "It was just tha—"

"We don't have time for this, Mary. Let's go. Straight down this way. C'mon." He didn't grab for her hand this time around. Mary knew she'd hurt his pride by touching him. There was still so much about Old World people she needed to learn. *Good luck finding some of them still alive. Hahaha,* the voice of the Palace director said from a place deep inside. They took off running down the cold and silent hallway of the basement.

The once beautiful plush green field of the rebel Palace now smelled of death. The grass kicked up into clumps of dirty, blood-soaked boot prints stretched as far as the eye could see. The killing field was littered with bodies, spent bullet casings, and pieces of the men and women of her squad. Of Logan's squad...the Eagle squad leader had trusted her, and what did he get for his troubles? A knife through the face and a squad full of dead bodies.

A part of her was happy he died there on the field before seeing what became of the squad she knew he loved dearly. It was a family he created, when they'd all lost the only families they ever knew. If she could speak to him one last time, she'd thank him for believing in her. But what would he think about her last orders to his group?

Mary was only doing what she thought he would have wanted—she'd fought, and she'd fought well. There were many dead members of the Palace-born squad, at least sixty by her own hands. It wasn't nearly enough when all was said and done.

Her fingers still felt numb from pulling on the triggers of too many guns to count. When one weapon emptied, she'd pick up another belonging to some unlucky soul. Then when the next weapon ran short of ammo, she'd throw it down to the crimson grass and quickly find another. At some point during her rage-filled murder frenzy, she'd shed the jacket given to her as a gift from Dale and Logan, slipping her arms out of the sleeves while flipping to retrieve some weapon. For the majority of the battle, she wore nothing but a white blood-smeared tank top and the Eagle squad pants.

The pattern of loading, unloading, ending one enemy, and then dodging another continued until multiple members of the Eagle squad had grabbed her, pushing Mary back inside the Palace. Even they could see the fight was over, but because she was okay to keep fighting, she hadn't noticed that the majority of the dead belonged to her own people. And, the sad truth was, she hadn't cared. In the heat of pure rage and vengeance, nothing meant more than dishing out fury.

Mary had been in a murderous state of hysteria, and she'd never felt more alive than when she was dancing around the bodies of the dead without tripping or missing a beat. Unloading clips, knocking limbs off with high-powered weaponry, becoming lost in her own world—she would still be out there trying to kill as many people as she could if someone hadn't stopped her. *It's who you are, Mary...I designed you perfectly*, the voice called again. She and Dale entered the crumbled remnant of the child center.

The first time she'd stepped into the child center there, she broke down in tears as she thought of the lost children stolen from her at another Palace, in what now seemed like another life.

Dale's only functional arm shot out suddenly to stop her. "Hold on,

I'm trying to remember where we go to get out of here." She could see his brain working, his fingers moving quickly, eyes darting back and forth. He was flustered and on the verge of panicking. Mary could even read his mind by looking deep into his optics. She would not make the same mistake of trying to comfort or help him. He would figure it out without her help; she knew he was more than capable. Overcompensation was the price of the guilty, and she felt plenty guilty. She partly wanted him to be wrong about the basement exit. Then she'd get a chance to go back out into the field. *And continue your work?*

"Umm okay, follow me." He began running toward the far-right corner of the child center. Mary followed close behind but stopped when something abnormal popped into her peripheral vision. It seemed to be a human hand. "Hold on, Dale." Mary slowly walked toward what she'd seen.

Dale abruptly stopped, spinning around in an odd motion, which she attributed to the dangling arm on his side. "What? We don't have time for this," he said, and he ran to gather her.

Mary smelled the dead man beneath the rocks before she'd actually spotted him. She knew it was the man Sirus spoke about in regard to someone Carla killed inside of the Palace. *I'd never tell such a filthy lie, you know me better than that, dear child.*

"I don't care about the dead body, we have to get you out of here," Dale said. He reached out to grab her hand. Mary turned to face him, pulling her hand out of his reach. The dead man under the rock brought her back into the moment. Reminded her of what she'd made of the second Palace she inhabited. She felt small, scurrying away like a rodent while others would never get the chance to leave. Their final resting place was the rebel Palace; why should hers be any different? Why should she get to live another day?

"Why!" she screamed at the young intel specialist of the now destroyed Eagle squad. "Why should I leave? I can do more. I gave the order saying we would fig—"

"We really don't have time for this, Mary. We have to leave. We can't die here—*you* can't die here. And you can't go back out there,

Mary...You really don't know what I mean, do you?" Dale asked with a troubled look on his face. Immediately he shook it off then moved close enough to grab her arm, clasping his hand around her wrist.

Mary shook loose like she'd done upstairs. "Don't touch me! You can leave if you want to get away. I was able to take down Sirus and his sizeable ship, and I can do more. I have to do more," Mary said as her eyes began welling up with tears. She was shaking while she spoke, not even sure if she believed what she was saying.

Running away wasn't the answer though. Every time she ran away, others ended up hurt. Jacob wouldn't leave people he cared for to die alone. She didn't necessarily care for the members of the Eagle squad as much as she felt responsible for their deaths. After all, she'd given the order to charge outside and engage in a firefight with the Palace soldiers.

They all died because she'd made the wrong decision. She heard what Sirus said about the perimeter of the Palace being a restrictor of their semi-superhuman abilities. She knew they were improved versions of the Old World members, but still, she sent them to die.

"If you die here, it was all for nothing! Don't you understand?" Dale screamed back at her. He took a step back from her and pointed at a boarded-up portion of the wall. "Please, the exit is right there up ahead. Let's just go, Mary. We can't allow you to die here."

"Where would you rather die, Dale? A mile from here? Maybe a few days from now? If we couldn't beat them with the full Eagle squad and this damn weapon, how will anything change when we run away?" Mary held the weapon up to his face and then threw it near the dead man underneath the immense rock. She immediately regretted her childish decision the second it left her hand, but her body was on fire with anger.

Dale ran over to the small piece of grayish metal to pick it up at once. "Are you stupid?" he bellowed. "This is the only thing giving us the slightest chance against the Order, and you take it and throw it on the ground as if you didn't see what it did to the ship out there on the battlefield. Don't compile mistakes. If you think you had a lapse in judgement by going into battle with the Order, you don't give in and die for the sake of trying to do the impossible, you live to fix it! Don't throw your life away. In order to fix the wrongs on the battlefield, you must live."

Dale walked back to Mary's side and slid the small weapon into her pocket. "Don't let the sacrifice be for nothing. Yes, we lost the Eagle squad here, but the world is likely teeming with hundreds, maybe even thousands of squads like ours. They need you as well. It's about more than what happened here today."

Mary had no idea why, but she wanted to hug him. She grabbed Dale and put her arms around his broad shoulders and began to cry. Her entire body trembled, the tears running from her eyes like broken faucets. All of the tension and pain melted from her body once she allowed herself to let it out. He was right, and she knew it. She hadn't been this upset when Carla's poison caused her to have a miscarriage. Going back would allow her to grant herself the death wish she'd had since losing her and Jacob's child—really since losing Jacob—a lifetime ago.

"Logan told me to get you away from the area if circumstances took a turn for the worse and success was not possible. I'm honoring my commander's wishes and giving you a chance to try again. He once told me you were the one who could remove this threat from our planet. He believed in you." Dale put his good hand on her shoulder, pushing her backwards and allowing them to look each other in the face. "We have to try, Mary. We will find others and try again. Please." Dale wiped tears from her eyes with the back of his hand.

Mary reluctantly nodded. With her head down, she walked toward the boarded-up spot in the wall with Dale. Nothing could be gained by continuing to argue with him; it would only lead to both of them being found and killed. She didn't care about her own life, but she did not want to see him die.

He tore the wood planks from the makeshift exit to open up their getaway route. Before leaving, Mary gazed over her shoulder at the dead man beneath the rock once more. Not because she cared for him particularly, but because he could serve as her last reminder of what took place there. What was taking place all over the planet.

She would use it as fuel to power what she would need to stop the Order. There was a warmth coming from the metallic weapon in her pocket. Its aura warmed her thigh, and it felt as though it were reacting to her once again. That helped to water down the hopeless feeling dwelling inside of her.

Dale reached for her. Mary grabbed his good hand, and together they entered what appeared to be a sewer system. "It leads to an abandoned neighborhood a few miles away. We will be safe there until we can figure out the next move." She knew there was no such thing as safe in their world; this day would serve as a reminder that she had to kill off any hope of harmony in this place. There would be no chance of peace as long as the Order was left unchecked.

DAVID

"I'LL BE TAKING OVER THE PALACE PROGRAM FROM HENCEFORTH. SIRUS is no longer available, and when he is…feeling better, he will be repurposed. Some of our kind tend to become overzealous in regard to their experiments." David sneered and clasped both hands together at his mid-section. "Sirus, as you know, was prone to such behavior."

There were fifteen teachers sitting in the front row of the auditorium. The same auditorium used to exterminate the Old World members. There was dim lighting in the massive space. The curtains behind the stage were dark red, nearly the color of blood left to coagulate over time.

No one spoke up; they knew questions would not be asked of them and opinions were not wanted. David stood at the podium like he had only months ago, when he came to speak on behalf of the Order after the man Dwight had killed a young specimen during phase 1 of the program.

"I had a mind to simply close the entire reality down and move on to other fruitful situations we have elsewhere, but some of the other members of my sect decided that *this* experiment was worth seeing through to the end. Friends of Sirus, I suppose." He surveyed the room, scrutinizing the teachers with his eyes. Judging them with a stare, he was curious if they could feel his contempt. David's feminine features painted a face of disgust as he spoke about the planet as a whole. His face was clean-shaven and shined in the lone light beaming down on him from the ceiling. He looked as if he were getting ready for some considerably important performance there on the stage.

"You would think that after three or four failed experiments, Sirus would move on to something else. I have my theories on that though. I want you to know there are exciting opportunities going on in other portions of the beam, or other realities, I should say. I know all of you are interested in the child portion of this particular program—you'd not be here if you weren't.

"I'm overseeing a different situation, allowing more of the embryo formatting, more customization. It's all going well and close to moving into its final stage. If any of you want to move into other programs in the coming pipeline, feel free to post out after the conclusion of this exercise, which I've decided to expedite for obvious reasons."

David unclasped his hands, forced a smile, and placed his hands palms down on the dark wood of the podium as he exhaled deeply. The smile vanished, and the stone-cold stare he'd become known for throughout his group appeared on his face.

"I'm ordering all Old World members in every Palace around this planet be eliminated. We have enough data to finish what Sirus started, without his constant meddling with the specimens. While the Palace-born are out taking care of the virus that's been keeping this experiment from completion for far too long, we will be meeting to discuss more matters NCP related. None of you are to leave the Palace for any reason. Learn from the mistakes of Sirus and allow the creations to do the heavy lifting. You are all dismissed."

MARY

DALE WALKED HARD, HARDER THAN SHE'D EVER NOTICED BEFORE. SHE didn't know if he was aware of it or not. For a soldier, even working in intelligence, he was as flatfooted as they came. He was excited to get away from the rebel Palace and get to the promised neighborhood somewhere above. She had no idea what they would do then, but it was the only plan they had. She supposed it was better than running into battle and dying...the thought was still heavy in her mind. Dale was right, regroup—come up with a plan and try again.

This can all stop if you go back and give yourself to the Order...don't delay the inevitable, Mary thought to herself. Or was it Sirus saying it to her? Didn't matter. If what he said was true, they were one and the same. The Order would like that, wouldn't they? If she ignorantly came running back to trade her own life for false promises. Wouldn't matter anyway, even giving herself up would not replace the lives lost. Nothing could bring them back. The only thing left was payback.

"Keep up, we are almost at the end here." Dale pointed into the dark sewer ahead as if either of them could see what was there.

"Don't worry, I'm not going to run. I'm with you, Dale." Mary sped up to walk by his side. She noticed he was closing his eyes and frowning in pain. His arm was worse now than before and not getting better anytime soon. The poor thing drooped near his hip, banging off the gun clipped to his belt. Mary wanted to break off the dead arm— the banging sound bothered her. Now that she thought about it, the arm could be why he was walking so quickly and loudly. Dale needed medical help, and she needed to get her head back into the game. His status was not lost on her, but it was becoming increasingly harder to control her compulsion to fight...or kill.

6

LONNIE

HE AND TWENTY OF HIS BEST MEN AND WOMEN HEADED BACK TO THE
Palace later in the day. The others were ordered to clean up the dead
and continue searching for Mary. Somehow, she'd escaped the killing
field and made her way to safety. A cowardly but intelligent move.
The fight was lost the moment he and his unit showed up. He specifi-
cally surveyed every face of every dead body after the battle, even
those who had been killed while shooting from inside the rebel Palace
at his men. She was nowhere to be found.

Lonnie walked into his pod and closed the door behind him. The
air conditioning made the sweat on the back of his neck so cold that
goose bumps covered his arms and a chill went streaking down his
spine. The jacket he wore was heavy with perspiration and the day's
work. He removed the bulky article of clothing, which also had a
built-in chest protector made of Kevlar, and dropped it on the floor
next to the door.

He knew others would come to pick up the dirty clothing and have
it back to him within hours. Lonnie only needed to worry about
resting and thinking about the battles to come. There was more than
enough work to do, and he'd be back out there searching for Mary in
the morning. His squad and everyone else below the rank of captain

26

thought the only point in the battle was to kill off the rats, but he and a chosen few knew retrieving Mary was higher on the list of objectives.

There was a light shining bright on his nutrition dispensary. He stretched his arms to the ceiling as far as he could and took off the black shirt he'd been wearing beneath his jacket. Since becoming a leader of the Palace Military, Lonnie noticed how his body had begun to change. It was normal, he supposed. He did work out a lot. He hadn't expected to get as strapping as he had as fast as he did, but he wasn't complaining. There were dangers out there in the world, and he needed to be able to protect himself and his soldiers.

Lonnie clicked the *open* button on the dispensary to find a large canteen of ice-cold water. It's what he had ordered on the keypad before leaving his room that morning. Even then, he was confident they would win, that he'd be back there to drink the cold water. Speaking words into existence; Teacher Simon spoke of this when they'd talked about war, battle, and topics in that vein.

"If you don't believe in what you are doing, you have no chance of success. Believe in the Order ENTIRELY." Those were his exact words. To an extent he was right, at least in the case of war. Lonnie thought about it. Holding the canteen to his lips, he gulped the water down like it was the first thing he'd ever drunk.

Once he finished the canteen of cold water, he placed it back into the nutrition dispensary, closed the hatch, and clicked the *return* button. The food he ordered still sat inside. The meatloaf and mashed potatoes no longer sounded good to him; he'd witnessed far too much as of late to eat a meal with so much red sauce. The water was enough for now.

The shower called his name like a longtime friend. There was grime and blood all over his skin and hair. Now that his rage had subsided and he was back in the pod, the filth had become noticeable. Most of his close-range kills had not been clean. Not as clean as he would have liked.

Lonnie had trained hard for this day. The blood all over his clothes was the first testament to the fact that he still had much practicing to do. There would be time for that though, and there would be plenty of Old World members to eliminate. Teacher Luke filled him in on the new rules as soon as he'd made it back to the Palace. Total annihilation of the rats, regardless of phase—he liked the way that sounded. There was no doubt most Palaces could walk their rats into the proverbial gas chamber, but there were many rebel Palaces needing a good conquering, and that was his long-term purpose. At least until he could meet his ultimate goal.

The thought of more violence, more killing, and more honing his skill made him excited. He stretched his neck around in a circle, listening for a popping sound. "Ahh," he said aloud once he heard the lovely pop in the base of his neck. Lonnie kicked off his boots, walked over to the bed, and lay down. He wanted to think for a moment. To think about the day, and exactly what needed to be done in order to find Mary. Teacher Luke told him that before he could move on to other Palaces, he needed to first bring the current situation to an end.

For brief periods during the fighting, he'd caught glimpses of her mowing down his people. Her shooting precision was remarkably accurate; at one time he'd seen Mary shoot a gun nine times, and all nine bullets brought down nine of his people. For a while he only saw her. It had been nearly hypnotizing what she'd been doing, how she had moved, going on about her business.

One thing was for sure: she was very good at killing, unbelievably good at something she'd never done before that day, to his knowledge. In those moments, the dispatching of lives appeared as natural to her as taking in and releasing air through her lungs. She wasn't as good as him, he thought, but still good. And different. The way she moved was unique. Faster than anyone he'd seen, and it was hard to get a line on her. He had tried though, that was for sure—but to no avail.

Then there was the question of what she'd used to destroy Sirus's Lohar vessel. It took all of his nerves to not turn around when he saw the monstrosity burst into flames. The blinding beam of multi-colored flame came from her; he saw that with his own eyes. It didn't happen again when the battle began, so he wasn't sure if it was a one-time thing or what. Sirus paid the price so they all could be alive. If she'd used that power on his unit, they would all be toast.

How did she know the vessel was a part of him? How could she know it was where his life force was maintained? He'd been learning a lot about Sirus and the others, and even still, he didn't understand much of the lessons he learned. He knew enough to know that they were beyond the planet and could not be hurt in the same ways he could. Somehow, Mary had figured out a way to cause Sirus pain. Lonnie didn't know how she'd done it, but information could be valuable, just in case.

Since losing Melinda, he'd become something different. Thinking about her put him in a place that made him feel too vulnerable. He did the opposite of tapping into his emotions; the learned feelings meant nothing in this world—nothing did. He'd come to the realization that not caring was the safest way to live the life he'd be given. Instead, he threw himself into his new role and all matters pertaining to it. The hunger to hurt, be hurt, to carve out his piece of the New World—it was important to him. A lofty goal was a goal worth living for, and sometimes finding a reason to live was more important than said reason. Losing Melinda was his real-time teaching moment.

When all of the Old World members were exterminated, the teachers and the guys with the yellow coats (who made him uneasy) would be leaving, and the fate of the planet would lie in those who were strong and helpful during the current times, those who took the world back, giving humanity a second chance. There would be books written about him; he could be a god of sorts.

Lonnie closed his eyes and thought about the future he could have if plans ended up going in his favor and he could find Mary. The Order would look upon him in the best and brightest of lights. Finding her wouldn't be too hard. He even had an idea where she could be. By the time morning came, he would hear back from the small squad he'd sent after her and the friend she'd taken with her. Leaving one of the rebels alive to torture for information was a great idea. Lonnie rose from the bed to take a shower before meeting with his lieutenants. There were extensive plans to discuss.

7

MARY

THERE STOOD A PICTURE OF A FAMILY, A BEAUTIFUL FAMILY. SHE supposed the first family she'd ever seen would be beautiful to her, and for more than one reason. A family was something she'd never had the chance to be a part of or witness in her life. The time of families had ended long before she became an adult. At one time she thought this was a good thing. But no, she'd been brainwashed to believe such lies. Whether it was true or not didn't matter. She and every other Palace-born child had been denied the chance. That in itself was enough to desire redemption as far as she was concerned.

There was a father, a mother, and two children. There was a young man who appeared to be no more than eight or nine years old. He stood next to his sister, who appeared much younger, five years old or so if Mary had to guess. The boy had his arm around the sister in the picture. Mary could see how much love the family had for each other. They were all smiling, wearing formal clothes in front of a dark background. The mother stood behind the father with her elbow resting on his shoulder, while the kids stood off to the side, close enough to touch, but still to the side.

Mary lifted the picture, which rested inside of a gold-colored frame with cracks and rust, creating small map lines throughout. The frame felt thin and weightless in her hand, as if it could diminish into fragments beneath the weight of her fingertips. Dust covered the picture, which caused her to wonder how many days and nights the image of that family had stood there on the desk untouched. She tried to blow the dust away to get a better look at the family. She wanted to see if she recognized the mother or father; there was always a chance they could have been sent to her Palace if they survived the sickness. The dust proved to be too thick for the wind between her lips. Using her middle and index finger, Mary wiped away the gray powder, allowing it to accumulate on her fingers before brushing them along her pants. So much time had passed since the moment the picture was taken. The family there, smiling, loving one another, had no idea what was to come.

Dale left Mary in the home that they'd holed up in the night before. They'd come up from the sewer system into the abandoned neighborhood, just like he said they would. The place was utterly silent—a ghost of its former self. Even still, Mary was astonished to see a real Old World neighborhood. She'd only ever seen them in old pictures or on the videos they were approved to watch. Families, and those families who'd had their own houses to themselves, interested her. It had to have felt good to have privacy, but she could also see how that dynamic could breed isolation and misunderstandings over time.

Humans were a species needing that connection, needing each other. It was said that over the years, the people of the Old World became uncoupled, which caused the issues ultimately leading to their demise. Mary hated the Order and Sirus, but not everything they said was a lie.

Overgrowth from the grass sprouted up through the roads and sidewalks. The front yards were mini jungles themselves. Yellow weeds and thorny overgrowth were scattered throughout. Obviously, there was no one around to keep the lawns freshly cut or rein in the hedges. Without human interference, the world was meant to look exactly the way it currently did. She couldn't decide if the houses, roads, and other items from humanity were in the way, or if the overgrowth was the obstruction. Which was there first? Which was natural? The answer was easy to determine if the correct questions were asked.

Mary held the picture, looking at the family but not seeing them. She'd drifted off in thought about the town and the condition of their past way of life. Who should rightly own the planet? Nature or human kind?

Of course, I do, for I'm the creator of all you see, cannot see, and have ever known or could hope to learn—and you could own it as well, his voice answered.

The former intel specialist turned rebel was going house to house to find any type of provisions for them. Medicine, canned food, really anything that would help them on their journey and ultimately bide their time until Mary could learn to use the weapon given to her from Logan. His arm was getting worse since leaving the rebel palace. She noticed the limb hanging a bit lower than it had the day before. Even though he probably didn't notice, she could smell the infection seeping from beneath the makeshift bandage they'd made to go over the wound after digging the bullet out. With any luck, he would find some antibiotics.

She placed the picture face down. She didn't know why it felt right to lay it down that way, but it did. It made her feel like she was blinding them to what had become of their home, the lives they were promised but would never experience.

Mary walked away from the desk, making her way up the wooden staircase, her boots clacking loudly on the creaky wood. She walked slowly, holding on to the bannister that had also collected its fair share of dust over the years. The beautiful dwelling was now a crypt of no one, only memories forgotten.

The top of the steps showed four rooms. The sun of the early afternoon lit the entire floor, creating a shining reflection off the hardwood that stretched throughout the entire home.

Mary turned into the first room on her left. By the look of the toys scattered around, she immediately knew the room belonged to the little girl in the picture. She could again see the child's smiling face, long brown hair in a ponytail over her shoulder—but now she could see the child in the room. Running, pushing the little pink car along the wooden floor, dressing up the dolls to do whatever it was children did with such dolls after they were dressed. The thought again stirred hurtful memories in her stomach and displayed an image to her brain of the daughter she'd left in the Palace. Abandoned was a more fitting word, she thought.

The little girl she'd never met, the child she watched grow when time permitted though the two-way glass of the child center—that little girl was one of two children she wanted to push to the back of her mind. Another life, another time. That saying and thought process was becoming a convenient justification to not deal with emotions that were too hard for her to come to terms with. Everyone coped in their own ways.

There was a name spelled on the wall in huge plastic colorful font. Stick-on letters, she thought. There were similar items used on some of the walls of the child centers. Not to spell out names, but to label specific areas. The name spelled *Moriah*.

Her name was Moriah, that's beautiful, Mary thought while running her hands over a few articles of clothing here and observing other foreign objects there.

Eventually she opened the closet after stepping over what looked to her like a small tablet of some sort. The dark screen showing her reflection was dead, like everything else in the home. Dead like everything else in the town...or the world, for that matter. Hanging in the closet were many clothes: shirts, dresses, skirts, and pants. The clothes were a cascading color wheel of pinks, purples, light blues, and yellows.

The customary colors were symbols of the female gender in the Old World. Mary flicked through the clothes with her right hand while holding the closet door open with her left. She thought she could look through the clothes forever if that was an option. Surprisingly, even after years, the smell coming from them made her want to live in that room; it all felt so real to her, so tangible on a human level. Even though the experience of observing a home from the Old World felt absolutely alien to her, it also felt...right. If she had to choose a word to explain the experience she was having just then, it would be "right." Normal, even.

Mary did not want to get lost looking through only one room of the home; she wanted to see as much as she could before Dale came back with his worrying and his insisting that she practice over and over with the metal weapon. Which she was having no luck with, by the way. She could feel the object become warm from time to time, but she did not understand why or how. There would be ample time to worry about that later. Mary quietly closed the closet, placing both hands over the doors. Then she walked out into the hallway once more.

The room directly to the left of the little girl's room was a bathroom. Not much different than the one she'd had in the Palace. Mary poked her head inside to see a toilet, sink, and a stand-up shower. She decided that would be enough for her. Nothing special or unique to see in there, but there was a full room across the hallway. A very disorganized room, she thought. Had to belong to the young boy in the picture. The posters of men wearing sporting uniforms was the giveaway, among other boy-related belongings.

The boy's room was a tornado of clothes and small toy-men dressed in army clothing. Some of the plastic men were lying on the ground, and there were others sitting upright with eccentric clothing on. *Those are superheroes.* She'd learned about those types of pop culture ideologies in a morning enrichment class or two. Teacher Paul gave the lectures on the superhero topic along with other silly notions that humans wasted much time on, most of which were not based in reality. She could recall the lesson tying the superheroes to the gods of the Old World.

Looking over the room, taking in the many posters, toys, and pointless items people put their time into in the Old World, she finally remembered a particular lesson during morning enrichment class. People from that time romanticized the supernatural to the point that they created countless religions and belief systems on the ideas that they or their gods could hold some of those abilities at the ready.

There was a heavy belief in evolving to the point of being special. The sad part was, it could have been possible if they had focused on positivity, and not killing each other.

I recall you doing a fair share of killing just yesterday. Some behaviors never change, right? Hahahaha. Sirus's laughter faded off into a dark echo. Mary squeezed her eyes shut, putting her focus back on the room. She wasn't sure if she was more interested in discoveries throughout the house or simply keeping herself occupied so the voice of the creator of the Palace program did not drive her crazy with his constant heckling.

There was something worrying her though; Mary wasn't sure it was actually him and not her own voice. She remembered from her time in the Palace that the mind was powerful and could create most anything you needed in order to cope with trauma. Teacher Paul's lesson came back to the surface of her attention.

The old favorite teacher of hers said even the gods of the Old World were no more than small toys with special powers. Around to provide comfort and empathy, wielding powers men wished to possess one day. She picked up two of the toys and thought about herself and the other Palace-born. She wondered what those from the time before the sickness would think of them based on the battlefield of the rebel palace, which was now a furious abstract painting of slaughter, illustrating what happened when you put the old humans against the new.

The thought caused her eye to twitch. As she felt her temperature rising, Mary stopped pacing the room. She placed the action figures on a wall shelf and calmed herself down by counting to ten (something Dale had taught her to do) before sitting on the boy's bed. Between the voice in her mind that did not belong to her and the anger about what happened to the rebel squad, she was having a bad go of the day thus far.

The bedspread and sheets dangled halfway to the floor, exposing the bare mattress. Mary decided she would make the bed up. Partly to get her mind off of killing, and partly because of her own OCD about unmade beds. Living in the Palace made her unable to get comfortable on a bed if the sheets and comforter were not fitted correctly. Old habits die hard, and she had nothing better to do until Dale came back.

Mary lifted the mattress slightly with one hand and with the other began to smooth the fitted portion of the sheet beneath. That's when her knuckle skimmed a hard surface beneath the mattress. Mary lifted the mattress high enough to see what the object was and discovered a small book there. She dropped the sheet to the floor and grabbed the book before dropping the mattress and sitting down. There was a small boy on the cover of the book sitting next to a tree, writing in a book of his own. There was no title though. She'd never seen a book without a title, and it piqued her curiosity.

Mary flipped to a page somewhere in the middle. Each page was like notebook paper, the lines filled with writing. Not printed words, but handwriting from an actual pencil. *This is a diary*, she thought. She knew because Jacob had mentioned the personal books once when she was telling him about some of the nagging rules bothering her about the Palace so long ago.

Rules that caused feelings and events that kept her up at night. While holding her after sex one night, he told her that in the Old World, many girls or teenagers had diaries. Some even had locks on them. They were like little books that were used to record secrets with the written word. It now seemed that even young boys had diaries in the Old World as well. She wanted to know what secrets were left behind in that small book belonging to the smiling boy in the picture downstairs. Mary began reading the page she'd flipped to randomly.

Friday night.

I'm glad that dad is gone to work in alebama for the weak. Mom and Moriah and me are goin to get ice cream at the mall tomorow. We get to have fun with mom like that wen dad is gone to other states for work. and he wont be here to tuck us in bed. I really hate wen he does that. Ill be up all nite tryin to think about wich ice cream I want to try tomorow.

Good night to me.

Mary's lips slightly parted as she smiled at the pages. She

wondered what it would feel like to have a father and mother to do activities with her. Take her to get ice-cream and tuck her in at night. *I'll tuck you in, Mary. Come home to me*, he said from a place deep inside. He'd been interrupting her thoughts, saying nasty, pesky statements to her since their encounter on the field. She was not sure if he was dead; she doubted it, but there was a chance. Regardless of whether he was gone in the physical form or not, he most definitely lived on in her mind. Mary pushed his voice to a back room in her brain and continued to read. She flipped another few pages to the right.

Tuesday Morning

Dad screamed at mom all nite last nite. I could not get to sleep, so I sneaked into Moriahs room cus I know she would be scared to. When dad scream at mom sometimes he hit her in the head to make her listen to him. Moriah and me got under the cover. She fell asleep before me so I stayed up to listen to why they were fighting.

Dad was saying he just wanted to tuck Moriah in like he does to me. He said she was old enough for it. Mom cried and told him no, that enough was enough and she said she would tell the police man if he tried to go in her room and do it. I think mom should tell the police man that he tucks me in all the time. I was glad that dad did not come into Moriahs room last night.

Mary's smile broke apart after reading that entry in the diary. Why would the young boy not want his father to tuck him and his sister in at night? Seemed like a loving thing that any parent would do to make their child feel protected for that time in history. The time Mary had spent in the child center was enough to let her know that small children needed that comfort. In a lot of cases, their very lives depended on it.

The entries mentioned about the father hitting the child's mother on the head worried Mary. To think that the children were being exposed to such violence at that age was a bad thing developmentally for them. She wanted to read something more pleasant before putting the diary down and moving on to the next room. Again, Mary turned the page to read the next entry.

Monday night

I'm feeling alot better today. Went to the park with Janson and mikey, we had so much fun, I could not ride my bike because it hurt to much but we threw the ball around. I hope I make the football team this year to play quarter back.

I miss grandma and grandpa alot. She cook so good and mom is always happy when we are there. Dad doesnt come over to there house ever. Him and grandpa always argue about when he hit mom. I hope I get to go back over there soon. I got some good news to. Dad talk to me today and he said that he would not come touch me at night to tuck me in anymore. But he said that to me before and he did it again, so I don't know if I can believe him.

She closed the diary, and for a moment she thought about what she'd read. Some of the writing confused her—she had a feeling it was because she still didn't quite understand the ways of those that came before her. Especially Old World humans who had lived out in the world. The diary belonged back in its rightful place beneath the child's mattress. Mary returned the book then sat back down on the bed.

It felt good getting a chance to get an inside view into the world of a child living in the Old World before the sickness. The father of the house did seem to have an issue with being violent to the mother. That was something he needed to work on, but he did love his children. Hopefully it was something they were all able to work through over time. Mary wondered if they were together when the world decided it no longer wanted to play along in the game of housing, feeding, and quenching the thirst of billions.

There were no bodies in the house they were currently staying in. Dale warned her that they may find the dead still in some of the homes. So far, she'd found no remains or evidence of the deceased. Maybe they were at the grandparents' house when it all happened, or possibly out in one of the many cars that came to a dead stop in the middle of the road.

Thinking about the many Old World people reduced to bone in the neighborhood began to make her feel dirty; her skin itched and felt clammy. Mary rose from the bed, made a right, and walked into what had to be the parents' room. No teen posters or pictures of athletes, no toys strewn about the floor. Only wooden dressers, a freshly made bed, and a footstool at the bottom of the large bed. The room was darkened by the curtains pulled tightly shut in the windows.

Mary didn't want to pry in the room; she knew that it was best to leave that home on good terms mentally. There were elements the young boy had described in his diary that she did not understand, but the fact that there was abuse between the mother and father was enough to let her know that she should tread carefully.

There was a tall dresser to her immediate left upon entering the room—the kind with doors that swung open outwardly. She couldn't think of the name of the piece of furniture, but the word "armor" kept coming to mind. That wasn't the name, but it was close to that. Mary opened the door on the left, leaving the right side closed. There were shirts hanging up, nice shirts with the collars and buttons. The kind of shirts that the teachers wore beneath their suit jackets.

There was a good chance that if she continued to look through the room, she would find the mother's clothes, which would likely fit her much better and would be more appropriate. It didn't matter though, she only needed a shirt. The green pants with the pockets were staying; in a way, they still made her feel like she was a part of the Eagle squad, she and Dale being the last remaining members.

Mary grabbed one of the white collared shirts off the hanger before leaving the parents' room and heading into the bathroom.

For the next thirty minutes, Mary went out to the backyard area of the home where there was a pond with medium sized rocks surrounding it. Creating something that reminded her of the courtyard in the Palace. But, smaller of course. The memories came rushing back as she collected enough water in a bucket she found near the back door. She returned to the upstairs bathroom (not sure why it was important to wash up there) to get clean. So much of what she'd been through felt ingrained deep in the pores of her skin. It went fast but Mary felt better after scrubbing her skin clean, or as clean as it was going to get.

Afterwards, she ran to the room she thought to be that of the parents, then guessed the right drawer, the one that held the mother's panties. Mary grabbed a blue pair, slammed the drawer shut, slipped them on right then and there, and made her way back to the bathroom to get dressed.

She didn't know why, but the parents room made her feel uneasy. Could have been the darkness, but something told her that bad memories still lingered in that room, more often than the young boy from the diary even knew.

C'mon, Mary, you are a smart woman. For all that you have seen good in the Old World people, you have seen and will see so much worse from them. At some point, you will understand why I had to do this, and why you must help me.

Slipping back into her pants, which did have some blood and dirt stains on them—Mary thought about what the voice in her mind said, the voice that sounded like Sirus, but also like herself. The part about her helping him was nonsense; she would not think on that. But there was something to the words about Old World people being both good and bad...but, were they mostly bad? Was she majority bad? The thought never crossed her mind in such a way, but now that it had, she felt perplexed. There was truth to it, but did it even matter?

Mary thought not. No...it didn't matter. At least not now, and not to her. There were people needing her help in the world, and there was a double dip involved because her helping others would also hurt the Order. Anything involved in hurting the Order the way they'd tried so hard and succeeded in hurting her would be high on her list of things to do.

The man-sized white dress shirt she now wore felt like a night-gown. The sleeves were not much longer than her own arms, but the body of the shirt was billowing out in every direction. There was a positive to such a considerable top though; she didn't feel restrained at all while wearing it. Her arms could move around more freely. Mary stretched her arms into the air and yawned, then sat down on the toilet and slipped her boots back on.

She thought it would be wise to go back downstairs and wait for Dale. The thought crossed her mind to go out looking for him. He'd said not to, but it had taken him long on what he claimed would be a short errand.

That's when she thought she heard Dale walking into the house. Fast footsteps and the rustle of heavy clothing sounded from downstairs.

But then, she realized an extra set of footsteps accompanied the first. No way Dale would bring a stranger back and not verbally call out to her before entering the home. He was just as on edge as she was. Mary slammed the thoughts she'd been pondering into the back of her mind and shot up from the toilet seat. She quickly ran across the white-tiled bathroom floor and out into the hallway. She made sure to keep her weight balanced so that her steps would not be heard from downstairs.

Mary felt calm and excited at the same time. She knew those inside of the home were not friendly, and she had a good idea about who the footsteps belonged to as well. There was a bit of worry in her mind as to where Dale was or if he was hurt, but that was not known and could not be answered until the threat below was taken care of.

She waited at the top of the steps just off to the side so that she was out of view. Someone began making their way up the steps, and Mary heard a slight clicking sound. She realized that was the sound of the safety being turned off of a small SMG. Without her own gun, which she'd left on the kitchen table, she knew that if a fight ensued, she would be up against these guys with no firearm to even the odds. She grinned as her body tightened and burned hot with opportunity. Mary's hand found the blade in the top left clip of her pants. That would do just fine.

8

BRANDEN

BY THE TIME HE'D MADE IT TO WHERE THE BODIES LAY COLD, THE majority of the participants were either dead or dying. Branden watched some of the final moments of a few poor souls staring up into the full clouds of a now beautiful sky. Their final resting place was to be a blood-soaked battlefield. Some were still coughing up blood as they knocked on death's door, requesting entry. Missing the obvious fight was fine by him; he was more into tactical, one-on-one assaults—no more than three at a time. The amount of bodies, weapons, and spent shells splayed all around the grass told the story of an event for which he would be best suited to stay on the sidelines. By observing, knowledge could be gained.

He'd learned much about war from his father, who fancied himself a historian of sorts. He would say, "When the world goes back to the old days, there will need to be people who still remember the history of the old world."

Living in a different home every thirty days left plenty of time to search for as many books to read. The types of books that allowed him to speak intelligently about things the only two adults he knew had interest in. He and his father would go hunting or simply walk and talk in the woods. That was the time they had to discuss topics such as politicians and the wars of old. Branden didn't care for the subject, but it meant so much to his father to have someone to speak to about adult topics that he pretended to enjoy it. But, not enjoying a lesson didn't mean you could not learn.

Branden sat and observed from a place where he could remain invisible to any eyes in the area. The victors walked in and out of the humongous building in the not so far distance. He watched the battle-field from the shrubbery no more than fifty yards from the closest body to him. The woman was still alive, but she didn't have long. Unfortunately, she'd taken a bullet to the stomach, and he could see that her system was shutting down. That process could be a long and painful one though; he knew this from personal experience.

Branden could possibly make it over to her and end her suffering before one of the scouts made the rounds back to that area, but why risk it? He knew that ending all suffering for those that had a longer wait to die was not possible, and she was no one special to him. Branden decided to stay where he was in order to attempt a surprise attack on one of the scouts the next time he came around.

The particular soldier carried a large gun, a helmet, and other combat gear. He was not very large in stature, but neither was Branden, which meant a knife would be the best option. In his mind, the knife was always the best option. It held a certain special place in his heart. After all, the blade was the first instrument he had used to take a life. Guns were loud and drew attention; he needed quiet and elusiveness.

The knife clipped onto the side of his jeans had been freshly sharp-ened the night before. Even though he had cut the throats of the men earlier that day, it should still be sharp enough for more work. Branden pulled the knife free and waited. The sun was high, the weather was good, and he had nothing but time. Hunters waited for the right chance to leap onto their unsuspecting victims. So, he'd wait —while the dead and injured men and women also waited for their time to die.

9

LAWRENCE

"IT'S THE ONLY WAY I CAN IMAGINE THINGS GOING BACK TO THE OLD days without a hitch. I've heard whispers pertaining to the 'outside' becoming safe again," Lawrence said, lifting one eyebrow and popping another green grape into his mouth. He bit down on it with his back teeth while listening to the replies and rebuttals of his two closest friends.

Lawrence wasn't sure if the rumors were correct or not. And really, it didn't matter to him. Some gossip was better than no gossip, and in a place like the Palace, any topic was a worthy topic. Especially the "forbidden ones." After twenty years of being in one place, you learned to make do.

They were not supposed to have groups or specific friends, because they were all family, blah blah blah. Those were the teachings, and he understood why ideals were being retaught that way. At the same time, it was hard to teach old dogs new tricks, if not impossible altogether. He'd always thought the idea of trying to reprogram fully grown adults how to love, nurture, and communicate was mission impossible. Of course, they could act well enough, pretend and go through the motions, but they would forever be exactly what they were. For better or worse...obviously worse in this case.

"Is that a fact, Lawrence?" Gregory James, who was also into his twentieth year in the Palace at age forty-three, said in a whisper. "You mean, like we may be able to leave this place at some point? Like, without the Greater Understanding Program? That doesn't make sense though. Why put us through all of this for so long just to release everyone all willy-nilly?"

Lawrence simply raised both eyebrows and gave a "you never know" look to his long-time friend.

"Who knows, Greg? I wouldn't put anything by these teachers." Lawrence popped another grape into his mouth. "I don't care either way, to be honest with you. I've come to enjoy this place. Don't have to work or worry about much of anything. I'd just as well stay in here if they were to give us the option of leaving or staying."

At the age of fifty-four, Lawrence Ingles was by far one of the more knowledgeable Old World members in Palace 57, which was located in a heavily wooded area of Beatrice, Nebraska. He and his late wife, Pamela, had owned a home in La Vista, not terribly far from his current location. She didn't make the trip to the Palace, and neither did his son, Michael. Over time, he'd learned to come to grips with the fact that he was truly alone, even if he was held up in a utopian (but not really) facility with over five hundred other people. None of those people truly knew him or everything he was about.

Billy Maddox sat back in his chair, looking unimpressed at the idea of being free to go back out into the world. Billy and his son had made it into the Palace as the lone survivors of their family, which was not massive to begin with. A few cousins here, an aunt or uncle there. Billy's son, Brady, was now thirty-one years old. His son took more to the teachings of the Order than he or any of the older members did. Much easier to brainwash an eleven-year-old child.

Lawrence popped a few more grapes into his mouth, nodding in agreement with Billy.

"I hear ya there. We do have a nice little setup going on here. I was more so just repeating what I was hearing; you guys know I've always had a hard time holding my water." The men laughed together at the joke. "My source says that's why Sirus stopped coming on the television for dinner." He lazily pointed at the TV embedded in the wall. It read "Please Wait."

Gregory stood up from his seat, grabbing the cup of cider he'd been drinking. "I'd love to get back out into the world. I mean, if what you are hearing has any type of truth to it." He took a sip of his drink, looking up at the ceiling. "Wouldn't it be great if we could simply ask a teacher without the fear of being reprimanded like children or made to feel we are crazy?" he said, but it ended up sounding more like he was speaking to himself than to each of them. Lawrence could tell he was seriously pondering the possibility.

"Fuck around and get sick out there...I'll pass," Billy said with a smile. He playfully slapped Gregory on the back from his seated position, causing Greg to spill a bit of the cider on the front of his shirt.

"Dammit, Billy," Gregory said. He set the drink back on the table and grabbed a napkin, spit on one end, and then furiously wiped at the small stain on the front of his white polo shirt. "Not so hard, you big lout!" They all laughed together again.

The three friends sat and talked, like they did most days. Not all the topics were so hush-hush, but really, it didn't matter. Since coming into the Palace together, they'd taken a liking to each other; same as most of the Old World members. For a long time, they only had each other to talk to, to share their griefs.

Now there were Palace-born folk who were old enough to have adult conversation with, but just barely. Even then, there was a certain understanding of the world, morality, and experience that could not be learned in a classroom. That was the only type of "knowing" the Palace-born people had experienced.

"Probably no truth to it, I suppose. Just running my mouth. I mean, we been in here for over twenty years. I have no reason to think they are going to let us just leave without reaching that ever-elusive Greater Understanding goal." Lawrence stood up from his chair and collected his empty bowl. He headed over to the nutrition dispensary, popped the latch up, and placed the bowl inside.

Gregory walked toward him slowly, still wearing the face of a man deep in thought. It was no secret that Greg wanted out of the Palace. He'd had a hard time of everything that had happened with the sickness; some men would never come to terms with the past. Greg was known for constantly having issues with adjusting, repeatedly being sat down by the teachers for minor but troublesome violations. And every time he came back to them fragile and broken by the teachers, his two friends would bring him back to life with stories of the Old World and something as simple as a hug. A lot of times, that's all a man needed—to know that someone cared.

"But who told you that? I mean, there could be something to it. Everyone's been thinking that something was going on, with what you said about Sirus and such." He brushed the yellow stragglers of hair from his forehead, pushing it back up to the crown of his head, which was beginning to bald.

"A man never tells all of his secr—"

Lawrence didn't get all of the words from his mouth before the television interrupted the talk he was having with his friends. BEEEEEEEEP, BEEEEEEEEP, BEEEEEEEP, the television screamed. All three men nearly jumped out of their skin. They'd never heard such a sound from the TV. The bold white words "Please Wait" no longer shined bright against the darkened background. They were gone, and what replaced them was, "Emergency, stay in your pods. There has been a breach." BEEEEEEEP, BEEEEEEEEP, BEEEEEEEEP. Over and over.

"What the hell is that?" Billy said, finally getting to his feet and joining his friends near the TV. They all peered back and forth at each other and the television, no one knowing what to say.

"Something about a breach. I don't know what that means, but it says stay in the pod, so that's what we are gonna do, right?" Lawrence said, unable to look away from the words on the TV. He knew that something was wrong. Too many oddities were happening in too short of a time. The Palace was nothing if not regular, consistent, and boring. He'd always been good at talking monster-sized issues into much smaller ones, for his own sanity. That's how he overcame the mind-fuck of the sickness and the trauma of losing everyone. Finding the silver lining was his thing, if he ever had one, but he was not dense —and would not pretend to be.

"That's weird though, Lawrence. Who would come here? Who could even exist out there to come here?" Gregory's eyes darted away from the screen, looking directly at Lawrence.

"Hell if I know...I wouldn't leave if I were you two though. It says to stay. I know this isn't your pod, but I think they mean to not be wandering the halls or on the elevator. Maybe they're trying to catch someone." Still, Lawrence did not look up from the television, as if staring at it would make the words change or go away.

"I'm going back to my po—" Billy didn't get a chance to finish his sentence before a loud knock at the door cut him off. KNOCK, KNOCK. The sound was loud, all knuckle.

The color drained from each of their faces as they looked left to right at one another, wondering which of them would be brave enough to answer. Unsure of what to do, finally Billy said, "Open the damn thing." He nodded his head at the door, peering at Lawrence. "It's your pod, man."

"Shhhh," he said, his skinny index finger shooting up to his lips, signaling them to be quiet. Lawrence was afraid to open the door. He knew there was no reason to be afraid, but something told him to stand still and wait. Let the knocker move on to another pod. Maybe they would think he wasn't in his room. *Why would you want them to think you aren't in your room?*

Lawrence wondered if he could somehow get in trouble for having Gregory and Billy in his pod. Normally it would be okay, but there were clearly changes afoot in the Palace. Anyone with eyes could see that, and he'd never been mistaken for a blind man.

Billy moved closer to him. "You gotta open the door. It could just be teachers or security checking up on us," he whispered.

Lawrence looked to Gregory for some type of signal that would decide the vote.

They were deadlocked. Greg nodded in agreement with Billy.

"Open the door, I'm sure it's nothing," Greg said in a low voice. He was chewing on his fingernails like he was apt to do when he was nervous. It was a tick that even the Palace could not rid him of. "Old World problems," he'd always say when his friends caught him chowing down on the nubs that were once his nails.

"I guess you are right," Lawrence said, reluctantly backing toward the door while still looking at his friends, both of whom appeared to be ready to push a load right then and there. He turned to face the door, slowly grabbed the knob, and turned it. Lawrence slightly cracked the door to look out into the hallway. There stood a security officer on the other side in full uniform.

"Is everything okay, sir?" Lawrence asked, only showing half of his face behind the door.

The security guard did not move to step inside. "I'd like to come into your pod to ask a few questions based on a security issue we are having." The guard spoke with no urgency in his voice; his tone indicated he'd been going door to door, asking the same mundane questions. Questions that he'd gotten the same answer for ninety-nine percent of the time. This put Lawrence at ease a bit more. If the guard was not urgent in his questioning, it couldn't be a big deal. There he was again, searching for that silver lining.

He opened the door entirely for the security officer, who was holding a handgun down at his side. That wasn't too off-putting— there was an issue going on, so that made sense to Lawrence. Gregory felt differently. The second he saw the gun in the security officer's hand, he walked backwards until his back touched the table, nearly knocking over one of the chairs. "Why...why's the gun drawn, sir?" he asked, pointing at the pistol.

The guard ignored Gregory. "Have a seat, everyone. Right there on the couch." He pointed at the white sofa next to the table and chairs. "I just have a few questions. Let's not make this harder than it has to be. Everyone is getting the same set of questions. Don't make me nervous."

That was a weird thing for the guard to say, Lawrence thought. *Why would he be nervous, and why does that matter? Nervous about what?* Beads of sweat sprouted from his forehead, and he could feel his armpits beginning to sweat as well.

All three men took a few steps over to the white sofa. They sat down, squeezing in next to each other. Lawrence knew they had to be as afraid as he was, if not more. Gregory was by nature a nervous person, and Billy was skeptical about everything. The thought crossed his mind that maybe they'd heard what he said to his friends about being set free with the Greater Understanding Program. That didn't make sense though; today wasn't the first day he'd said something along those lines.

He was old, but not old enough that his ears no longer worked. His TV was going off with the beeping sounds, and so were the TVs next door to him on either side. The sound was so loud, he couldn't help but hear it. That told him that it wasn't a personal thing toward him. Maybe they did just want to ask a few questions, and the guard that came to his door was of the nervous variety.

"Ask us anything, sir. We would be happy to help with anything at all." Lawrence placed his hands on his knees and awaited the questions from the security officer. The two men sitting next to him were a ball of nerves. Billy was visibly nervous, and Lawrence thought he would get up and run—probably would have tried if the guard wasn't closest to the door. And Gregory had tears in his eyes. They all knew something was wrong. Something had gone terribly wrong, and it was all coming to a head right there in the pod.

"Is there anyone else in the pod? In the bathroom maybe?"

"No sir, nobody. Just us three. We usually meet here in my pod to talk about this and that before dinner. It's just us, sir." He could hear his own fear. It made him ashamed for a moment, but he just wanted the situation to be over. He wanted to finish bullshitting with his friends and sit down for a nice dinner later.

"Good. Some things have changed here in the Palace, just today. I...I don't know if you all heard anything or something like that." He paused for a moment. "I don't know what I'm trying to say, really. I'm sorry, guys, I just have to..." The guard swallowed hard.

He was looking side to side, down at the ground, then back at them again, unable to hold eye contact for more than a few seconds. The security guard stammered, struggling to get the words out. "P-P-Plans have changed. They said that we have to do this."

Those words caused Billy to plant both hands into the couch to lift himself up. Lawrence had no idea what Billy had planned, but then it all happened. He watched it all, in shock of what he was seeing, unable to move or stop it. He wanted to say so much, he wanted to plead or beg for their lives. For all of their lives. Sometimes the moment was too hefty, or too fast for words. None of them ever had a chance to say anything at all. All four men had their fates entangled into a singular moment that was fixed. There were no words or intervention that could have stopped what was meant to happen. What was happening in every Palace all over the planet. Maybe not door-to-door shootings per se, but death, mass death—it was all the same.

Just as Billy stood up, the security guard fumbled the gun around for a split second— allowing a speck of a chance to enter Lawrence's mind. *He is going to drop the gun...then someone will do something. Not me, but someone.* That didn't happen though. The guard recovered control of the weapon, pointed it at Billy, and squeezed the trigger like his life depended on how fast he could get the bullets out of the clip. BOOM, BOOM, BOOM! Three shells at close range hit ol' Bill in the chest and stomach. The power from the handgun sat him right back down in the seat with such force that the sofa moved back an inch or two.

Gregory didn't try to run; the shock of what was happening froze him where he was with a spray of Bill's blood on the right sleeve of his shirt. He lifted both hands up to block his face from what was coming, and he knew it. A part of Lawrence thought Gregory's reaction to a gun pointing at him was hilarious, as if his stupid hands could block the bullets. Sitting there watching it all play out felt surreal, almost like he was watching a television show from back in the day. A crime thriller or something like that.

The reaction was actually a common movement from people who saw that physical harm was imminent. They throw their hands up to block whatever is heading their way: bullets, on-coming cars, a sword. The thought process that says your hands can stop any of those fatal events is laughable when you think about it outside of being in that moment yourself. Even still, when faced with those dangers, the hands go up. And like you would guess, they stopped nothing.

The security guard quickly set his aim on Gregory. BOOM BOOM! A bullet tore through the palm of his right hand, blowing it in half down to the wrist. To Lawrence, it looked more like an overgrown frog's hand without the webbing. The next bullet hit his friend beneath the eye, knocking off a piece of his high cheekbone. The flap of bone and skin swung around to the opposite side of his face. Gregory's body stiffened as his eyes rolled into his head, leaving his body sliding off the couch and onto the floor. Their bowels released upon their deaths—Lawrence could smell both of them, and it reminded him of the time he found his wife dead in bed the day of the sickness.

Lawrence only watched. He didn't try to run or have the time to register that his turn was next. Gregory was quick like that, always thinking ahead. Not Lawrence though; he was a man of the people, a talker, the type of guy others enjoyed being around because he had a knack for making everyone feel good about themselves.

No more than two or three minutes ago, all three men had been sitting at the table only a few feet away, bullshitting like they'd done for so many years before. He'd even had a bowl of grapes. A freaking bowl of grapes...who gets killed minutes after finishing off a bowl of grapes? Didn't seem likely at all, but somehow, he found himself in that exact situation.

He even still had some grape skin stuck in his back teeth, which he was trying to dislodge with his tongue, his body not quite realizing that his own number was being called.

Lawrence looked up to see the security guard's pistol pointed directly in his face. He saw nothing but the spacious hole of the firearm where a bullet, likely multiple bullets, would come from to send him to wherever his friends were. The guard's eyes were as round as tea saucers, and it occurred to Lawrence in the final moment of his life that the man did not want to do the job he'd been tasked with carrying out. But all men had a job to do, and all too often in the

Old or New World, those jobs entailed either killing or being killed. Maybe it was not so bad to be on the latter end of the equation. Lawrence and the guard locked eyes just as the hammer slammed down multiple times, disengaging two slugs that took off two-thirds of Lawrence's face.

MARY

FOR MARY, BATTLE ALWAYS PLAYED OUT LIKE A DANCE. WHETHER SHE was doing the killing or watching it happen, everything slowed down to a crawl. Then her legs began the business of pivots, leaping, sliding, running, and evading. Though she'd never learned such maneuvers, her feet would take the responsibility of the decision-making from her brain and go on autopilot. With each movement she made, it felt like a slow-down meter filled itself. In other words, the enemy became slower as the battle raged on and, more importantly, she became faster. At a point, Mary's enemies became sitting ducks.

Mary waited, crouched around the right corner at the top of the steps with her eyes closed. She rubbed the handle of the knife in her hand, feeling the smooth wood against the padding of her fingers. Nothing in life had ever made her feel so excited outside of being with Jacob in bed. She compared the feelings because fighting...even killing —they felt like a sexual high to her. Not exactly the same, but very similar. She found herself lost in the passion of it, the realness. That feeling did not exist before Jacob or after him, until the day prior. The day she'd taken many lives and escaped her own death time and time again. Nothing was more real, or more final. Mary did not know what being outside of the Palace was doing to her, but she knew it was changing her.

Eyes clenched, she thought about the dead Eagle squad members. Logan, the leader of the squad who gave his life trying to fight for what he believed in. She thought about Jacob, who died under the same type of circumstances. How many innocents from the time before had to die like animals to appease the Order, to appease Sirus?

All of them...you know that, Sirus said, but this time Mary did not push his words from her mind. For the first time in a long time, she agreed with him...they all *did* have to die. Not those from the Old World, but anyone working with or for the Order. She would not rest until that was the case.

Mary's eyes flipped open as she heard someone's foot creak against the wood on the steps. The Palace soldier had made it halfway up, and that was too far for her liking; he would not get the chance to lessen her position advantage. She sprung from the crouched position, vaulting off her feet onto the wooden banister against the wall of the staircase. The young soldier, who wore an eyepatch and looked no older than fifteen, glanced up at her. Slowly, his gun began moving up with his vision. At that moment, the world became silent for Mary—everything inside of her body felt as though it had been set aflame, and the slow dance began.

Mary's long hair, no longer in a ponytail, lifted with her as she took to the air, flowing behind her like shiny black threads of a deadly spiderweb. The toes of her right foot barely touched the bannister before she used the wall to support her weight, pushing off with her right hand. She landed on the right side of the young but deadly soldier.

The gun in his hand activated as he squeezed the trigger, riddling the stairway walls and ceiling with bullets. Clumps of drywall flew from where the bullets hit, littering the hardwood floor and steps with small white specks and larger chunks of the debris.

Mary was too fast though. To the soldier blindly swinging his firearm over his head trying to hit her, it had to feel like trying to shoot a housefly with a cannon ball. He never had a chance. While he was indeed skilled and very fast by normal standards, his attempts were for naught.

Mary's back ended up against the wall to the right of the young man. She stabbed her knife into the wall with her left hand, allowing her to hang in midair. Her left foot kicked the butt of the gun up while he was still shooting like a mad man. The movement occurred so fast, he didn't have time to register that the barrel of the gun was now aimed at his own face while he laid on the trigger.

And just like that, he was gone. The crackling of the bones in his face sounded as loud as the burst from the gun that had caused it. Two of the bullets hit his face, one disintegrating his chin just like the plaster in the wall only seconds before. The other bullet clipped his right cheek, tearing through the skin and sinking into the ceiling.

Before the gun hit the wooden steps along with the crumpled body of the teenaged shooter, Mary was back on her feet at the bottom of the steps, staring at the giant woman who stood in the doorway of the kitchen with a pistol in her hand. She had to be six foot two, at least. The female soldier looked slightly older than the boy, but not by much. She sported a buzz cut, that which Mary had only seen among men out in the world. It was fitting for her appearance though, if not for the long eye-lashes, angular shaped face and of course the breast— Mary could have easily mistaken her for a man.

Neither of them said a word. There was nothing to talk about, and they both knew what was to come. Mary knew the young girl was afraid—the look on her face said she wanted to run out the door. The time for leaving was long gone. Mary took a step to her right just as the boy's body slid down the final steps, coming to a rest on the floor. His legs were propped up on the final three steps. Mary knew she looked crazed, like a rabid dog—because she felt that way. She felt as though his death had given her life—all death dealt by her own hand made her feel more powerful.

The woman she had been so long ago in the Palace with Jacob was inside of her somewhere deep down…crying out. That part of herself was ashamed, not so much about killing in self-defense, but because she was *enjoying* the killing as much as she was. What she was becoming was something different altogether compared to what she truly was or had been. Or had she always been a killer? *You are so much more. You were created perfectly, even though there may be collateral damage when you erupt. It's all so beautiful just the same,* he said in her mind.

Mary moved on the woman near the kitchen with blinding speed.

The soldier from the Palace nearly jumped out of her boots when she realized Mary was close enough to touch her, even though she'd been five steps away just a split second before. No time passed between those two moments. The woman dropped her gun, either from fear or because she was smart enough to learn from her partner's mistakes.

There was a chance arrogance played a part, because the soldier tried grabbing Mary, but missed and stumbled instead. What she had been grasping at was now slightly behind her. A loud scream from the woman echoed throughout the home as Mary's knife landed between the ribs of the soldier with precision. She didn't even bother to remove the knife from her victim, and with a spin, Mary placed her arms around the woman's neck with the intention to choke her out.

No, break her neck, Mary. She's nothing compared to you. Feed the monster, Mary! END HER!!

The voice caused Mary to hesitate, and that was enough time to allow the immensely strong soldier a chance to counter. She moved her hand behind Mary's head, flipping her over her shoulder and onto the floor. The sound of the fight came bursting back into Mary's head as her back slammed against the wood floor, knocking the air out of her. Mary's eyes bugged in surprise at the strength of her opponent. A large boot was on its way down to her face.

Not nearly fast enough though, the moment of opportunity was over as fast as it began. Mary rolled out of the way of the boot, using her right hand to push herself up from the ground as her left hand swiftly scraped against the floor, picking up the handgun dropped by the Palace soldier.

By the time the woman's boot came down on the floor with a loud animalistic shout of rage, Mary was next to her with the pistol to her shaved head. Not only did the soldier not realize Mary was no longer beneath her boot, but everything happened so fast, she didn't even realize she now had a small hole beneath the opposite side of the rib cage where the knife still remained. Apparently, she did not hear the gun go off as well. The moment her boot came thundering down on the ground was the same moment Mary had already made it to her feet with the gun to the soldier's stomach, squeezing the trigger once before quickly shuffling backwards. The Palace soldiers also jerked back as she swung at Mary, but there was no recognition of being shot... not right away.

Mary recalled a lesson on death and its delayed symptoms in one of the Palace lectures. Not in all cases, but some. For instance, a chicken with its head cut off could continue running around for some time. It was as if the animal had no idea it was dead, and the nerves were going on about their business anyway. What she was observing with the female Palace soldier was exactly that. The woman had no idea she was already dead.

Mary stepped away from the woman, understanding the fight ended with that gun-shot. No matter how much the woman wanted to get to her, the wound would not allow it. She placed the gun on the fireplace mantel and watched her. The soldier whirled around with fury, her eyes full of rage as she moved toward Mary.

No more than a step or two, then she noticed the pain and warmth running down her right rib cage, transforming that portion of the white tank-top into a crimson stained piece of cloth. Blood ran down her stomach, onto her belt, pants, then dripped to her boots. Her hand quickly found the wound to touch it, to feel the origin of the fresh pain in her abdomen. She stopped walking to look at her bloody fingers. The rage on her face immediately transformed into shock and fear. The once monstrous, highly touted soldier of her unit morphed into a young girl— now forced to come to terms with the beckoning call of her own demise.

"What did you do to me?" The girl finally spoke, and with youthful fear in her eyes, she looked at the blood dripping from her fingers down to her wrist and forearm as she pointed at Mary with a trembling finger. "Did you shoot me? Why?" She took another step.

Mary watched her, knowing she would never make it to her before collapsing. A small part of her felt a painful ache deep in her soul for the young woman. A much more considerable portion of her felt elated with how the death was playing out. Slowly, painfully, and poetic in so many ways. A voice in her mind told her the soldier was getting what she'd given to so many the day before—she was getting what she deserved. What was once a small part of Mary was now beginning to take over every portion of who she was, and she agreed with that voice—it was true.

"Stop trying; just lie down and accept it. Death is now upon you, and there is nothing you can do," Mary said, speaking in the same voice as the man she hated more than anyone. The blood began to spurt from the wound like a sprinkler sitting on a nice lawn in the summer. The pupils of the soldier's eyes began to fade, moving upwards to the ceiling. She tried to babble about something, no doubt cursing Mary… or begging, pleading for her life. Unable to get words out, tears materialized from those hazy eyes, as she still reached out to Mary. Not to hurt her though—to be comforted.

There would be none for her though, not from Mary. The soldier fell face first to the ground, her face slapping against the hardwood like an oversized piece of raw meat. Mary took a step toward the body and bent down to lift the woman, but only to retrieve the knife still stuck in the now-dead flesh.

11

ZOE

Earlier in the day inside of Palace 178, just outside of Hong Kong in Shenzhen, Zoe experienced what she thought was the greatest day of her life. Every one of her friends were so excited for her. There were hugs, pats on the back, and some even gave her small gifts to remember them by when she left the child center forever—even though personal items outside of clothes were not allowed. The kids found ways to show their individuality when there were no watchers paying attention to them. Of course, they would see each other again in the pods, but who knew when that would be. No one knew their own birthday; only the watchers knew, and they only alerted the children of their transition to pod living when it was time.

One of the teachers retrieved Zoe from the child center with belongings in hand. He smiled, putting his large white teeth on display, and explained some elements to her he believed were important in adjusting to her new role, all of which she'd already forgotten. Then he showed her to her living quarters with the rest of the adults. Unlike some of the others moving from child center to the pods, Zoe was overjoyed by the opportunity in front of her.

It felt like a new world had become unlocked as she rode the elevator to the pod area. Where her life was once an open space in which many kids lived, worked together, and learned to survive, there were now many floors, many rooms, and much to do. Feelings of being overwhelmed consumed her, but she hid the notion from the teacher who accompanied her. He needed to know she was ready for her new life, because she was. It was a little scary at first, but she thought that was to be expected.

What she didn't know was that her world would get a lot scarier later that day. Actually, scary wasn't the word. There was no word for what she witnessed only hours after being out of the child center. The confusion coupled with never-before-seen violence was enough to make her crawl into herself and never come back out. They were killing each other...everyone. They killed each other without remorse or a second thought. One moment everything was fine, then the next thing she knew, people were dying.

Standing in the central plaza of her Palace, Zoe was frozen, watching it all. People were making statements she did not quite understand, screaming out hate-filled words as they continued their killing. Old World members of the Palace cried out things like, "Not again, we are not going to go willingly!" The security guards and what she thought were Palace-born humans like herself screamed back, "These are our orders. Go into the auditorium or die where you stand!"

There were knives, hatchets, machetes, and pieces of wood. Really, anything could be used to bring harm. The fighting persisted for what felt like hours, but only amounted to no more than twenty minutes or so. By the time it all ended, the floors were no longer the shiny white they'd been an hour before. Blood rose inches high, and she stood in it —unable to move.

Until a teacher, the same teacher who'd come to get her from the child center, found her standing there in the central plaza, shell shocked. Her long black hair hung over her face, hiding her look of pure horror. The long white dress she wore skimmed the bloody floor, and her white shoes were now red. The man placed a hand on her shoulder. She did not look up at him.

"Zoe?" He moved her head up to look at him by lifting her chin with his finger, which was also blood soaked. "Look at me?" he said once more before bending to a single knee to get eye level with her. "You don't have to be afraid. We have taken care of all those that would do you or the planet any more harm."

Still, Zoe could not look at the teacher. Her eyes were open and she was looking straight ahead, but she was not there. She had checked out after witnessing someone slitting the throat of an older woman just five feet away from her. The wound across the lady's neck was so open and wide that it seemed to smile at her, was laughing at her. Meanwhile, the face above the wound was the portrait of fear. For a child of ten years old, the images were too much. There had been two options for Zoe in that moment. Either she removed herself from the situation mentally, or she simply went mad. Both things could be true, and, in her case—they likely were.

The teacher tapped her on the forehead with his index finger. The pressure just above her eyebrows somehow brought her back to the moment in full effect. Zoe's eyes met the eyes of the teacher, his wide-set honey-colored eyes. The bright smile he'd shown earlier that day was no longer present. The look on his face was...boredom. Indifference maybe? To her that may have been worse than the violence she had witnessed. He stood up, grabbing on to her small trembling hand.

"Don't worry, young lady. We will fix you right up," he said to her as they walked over the bloody floors of the central plaza. Zoe slowly gazed up to him. The brightness in his eyes had returned, along with the grin on his lips.

1 2

BRANDEN

"What happened here today? And why?" Branden said, sitting next to the Palace-born soldier he'd jumped from the bushes, knocked out with the business end of his knife, and tied to a tree about a half mile from where the battle took place.

"I don't know any—"

"Ah ah ah," Branden said, just like his mother used to say when he was beginning to tell an untruth. "Okay, I'll talk first. That's only fair." He moved even closer to the tied-up soldier who seemed to be not much older than himself. No more than seventeen or eighteen years old. They sat so close that their arms were touching.

"I've done this type of thing…a lot. Well, maybe not a lot, but much more than you have. So, I'll explain the very simple rules." Branden lifted himself up a bit and quickly pulled his knife from the back of the jeans he wore. The blade performed a slicing, spinning dance in his fingers before finding a home on the leg of the soldier. Branden had made sure to pull the pants up to the thigh. As he mentioned, he'd been involved in such activities like this in the past.

The soldier was visibly upset. His face went red, and there were tears welling up in his eyes. Branden could feel him shaking a bit. "Don't you dare cry. You weren't crying when you were killing people earlier. Be the same YOU, regardless of the situation. Understand? A wise man once told me that." He laid the blade on the ground next to them. There was no fear of the soldier possibly laying hands on it, as his hands were tied behind him to the tree. His feet were also tied together, and Branden was exemplary at tying knots—able to make them as tight as a possible.

"Simply...don't scream or I'll cut your tongue out. Don't lie, or I'll start carving pieces out of your leg." He slapped the soldier's pale, hairy thigh. "If I think you are lying, I'll slice your face, and trust me, I'm pessimistic as fuck. Doesn't take much for me to think you aren't being straight with me. So, if I was you, I'd be really truthful. Get it?"

The soldier was staring at Branden like he was a monster. "I do, I do understand, and I'll tell you all that I know." He nodded his head up and down as fast as he could while staring deeply into Branden's eyes. "Can I ask you one question first?"

"Sure. Just one though. I have things to do." Branden grabbed the knife from the pine needle-littered ground.

"When we are done, can you please kill me quickly? I don't know if you planned on letting me go if I was honest with you or not, but I can't go back. They already know I've been captured," the soldier said with certainty in his voice.

"How would they know I have you? It hasn't been that long," Branden said with a confused look on his face. "If you are a good boy, I can have you back to them in no time. Depends on how honest you can be, and if I'm feeling nice afterwards." Branden scraped the hairs on the soldier's leg with the blade of the knife, causing him to jump in fear.

"No, no—you must end me. They know because he is always in our heads at all times. He knows what we are doing, and he knows what we are saying. Inside the Palace, he doesn't track us that way, but when we are out in the world. he knows." A tear fell from his eye. Those same brown eyes pleaded with Branden to give him death when they were done.

"He? Who is *he*?" Not knowing if the young soldier was lying to him in order to get him off his game, Branden shoved the knife to his throat. "Don't fucking play around with me, man. Who is *he?*" The soldier slowly lifted his head up and against the tree he sat tied to, exposing even more of his throat. Now, tears ran down his cheeks.

"Sirus, the Palace leader, the program director. I don't know how he does it, I really don't—but he is always in our minds. Speaking to us, saying things. Bad things." In that moment, his face was that of a child, a real child. Lost in a world that he'd only just come to recognize outside of the Palace. "Please, just promise to end my life."

"We will see how the talk goes. I'll consider it," Branden said. He had so many questions about who they were. Who was Sirus? What was the huge ship-looking thing that fell from the sky? Why were they fighting? They had time though, and he would get every answer he wanted. His prey was more than willing.

13

JONAS

"THANK YOU FOR BREATHING LIFE INTO EVERY MAN, WOMAN, CHILD, AND lifeform that you have deemed fit to walk on your skin, drink of your bosom, and eat of your fruit. We are thankful, and we shall never take your gifts for granted, O merciful Mother Earth. Amen." Jonas removed the napkin from his tray and placed it over his lap before grabbing the fork next to the grilled chicken he'd ordered for dinner that night.

Then Jonas placed the fork back on the plate and pushed the tray away. He'd been thinking about something all day. Saying the Earth's prayer pushed the thought back into the forefront of his mind. Not the words themselves—he didn't think anything about the words; he'd said them a billion times over. Those words held as much meaning to him as the fuzz balls on his socks.

What was bothering him was actually what they did *while* saying the Earth's prayer, which was saying the words with Sirus. For the last few days, there was no Sirus. That was weird. It was odd, and Jonas knew enough about the Palace and the world in general to know that skepticism was a gift, not a fleeting feeling.

If the only thing he had to worry about was Sirus not staring at them through the televisions, that wouldn't be enough to make him lose his appetite. God knew it had always been a weird thing, but it was what they were accustomed to.

Earlier that day in morning enrichment class, two of his friends were not present. He'd knocked on both their pod doors, but they hadn't answered. Neither friend showed up to work out or have an afternoon coffee, like they normally did.

Jonas hadn't eaten breakfast that morning because he was helping a few of the Palace-born teens with a project they were doing on Old World issues. He was one of the "oldest" Old World members in the Palace, and he took that seriously. Anything the youngsters needed to know (within reason), he would help them—and so he did. After doing that though, he'd walked to class alone. In the whole twenty or so years he'd been there in the Palace, neither friend ever missed a class without him knowing something about it. To someone else, those issues would not be cause for concern, but Jonas had seen larger events trickle down from smaller issues. He'd seen the world end before...and he'd seen worse than that.

He still needed to eat he supposed. Jonas again grabbed the fork from the plate. He picked over the green beans and grilled chicken. The food tasted fine—it was the same as it had always been. He chewed the food up, forcing it down his gullet. He knew that if he did not eat now, then he would wake up early wanting snacks. Pearl, another person from the Old World, made a comment about the weight he'd been picking up as of late. She was a sweetheart, but she had no filter on that mouth of hers. If times were different, he would court her and try to make her his woman. Old times, old ideas he knew—but his sex drive had died down some time ago, and just lying together and talking was enough for him now. He wished he could do that with her, but that wasn't allowed.

At the age of sixty-seven, small inconsistencies mattered more than the bigger picture. He'd learned that the "big picture" didn't exist. Life was made up of infinite small events, which in hindsight became "bigger picture" shit. Try explaining that to fifteen-year-old Palace-born kids who thought themselves adults with all the answers and aspirations of what they'd do after getting accepted into the Greater

Understanding Program. They had no idea what Germany was like before the sickness took it all away. Growing up in Berlin was unlike anything they could ever imagine. More than he could imagine as of late. Time had a way of stealing your memories from you in the night. You could go to sleep with the memory of someone's face or an event, then boom…you wake up and it's all gone.

Jonas sat back on the white sofa to ponder about his friends and what could be going on with Sirus and the Order. He knew something was coming. His throat was parched, as the only thing he'd had to drink that day was water from the fountains in the common areas. There was a cup of sweet tea on his tray, same drink he had every night. Reminded him of his late wife's recipe. It probably wasn't that close to her recipe, but again, time had a way of changing the norm on you. Jonas grabbed the cup and drank it all down without taking a break. That would do for dinner; he couldn't eat anymore, and the bed was calling his name. But before that, he wanted to go check on his friends once more before turning in.

Getting up from the sofa was a chore for Jonas. Like his friend Pearl said, he'd picked up quite a few pounds in his old age. After rocking back and forth a series of times, he found the momentum to make it to his feet. Jonas bent over to collect the tray of uneaten food, and that was when he felt it.

Even though he'd never felt such a thing, the pain going on in his chest was similar to someone with spiked gloves grabbing his heart and squeezing it like a stress ball. If that was ever a thing, it was what he felt the second he picked up the tray. The pain surged into his every nerve so fast that he lost all control of his arms and sent the tin tray toppling over to the floor along with the grilled chicken, green beans, and empty glass.

While the pain gripped his heart, Jonas tried to breathe and be calm. Maybe he needed to sit back down. Getting up so suddenly could have been the culprit behind what he was experiencing, but sitting down did not help the pain. He tried to breathe, but his throat was closing up on him. His nails began to claw at his throat, leaving bloody scratches on his pale, meaty neck. He didn't know what he was trying to do, but he wanted to breathe, and if ripping his own throat open to get some air was his only option, then that was his only option.

The sofa moved all around the room as Jonas lost control of himself. He flipped onto his back and side, scratching and trying to scream out for help. No sound would come from his mouth, nor did he have the strength or control of his legs to make it to the door.

By the time he gave in to what was happening, it was all clear to him. *They did this to me*, he thought. Lying there halfway off the couch with his throat a red, swollen mess, before the bright lights of his pod faded into darkness, he wondered: did my friends meet the same fate? He thought so.

14

MARY

W HILE MOVING BOTH BODIES INTO THE BASEMENT OF THE HOME, M ARY thought about Dale and why he'd not shown up yet. He said he would be gone for a little while and that she could find water nearby to bathe and find different clothes to wear. But, it had been over an hour since he left. The Palace-born soldiers that were most definitely hunting them had her worried. What if they had found him first? Fighting was not exactly his specialty, especially against people like them. That arm would be of no help if he did have to defend himself.

After pushing both bodies into a roomy closet in the basement, she began making her way back up the steps. That was when she heard something coming from outside. Coughing...it sounded like coughing. Mary took off up the steps, taking them three at a time before reaching the top. Darting across the living room floor, she carefully moved the curtains back from the window to see what was going on out there. Her first thought was to run outside, but there could be more soldiers out there waiting to get the drop on her.

There were no soldiers waiting to hurt her though; the two that had been sent were now packed in a closet downstairs. But, there *was* someone lying in the driveway of the home. She could tell right away that it was Dale. He lay face down with both arms stretched out, a bag next to him. The contents had fallen out, and some of the products were rolling down the driveway, which slanted upwards to the garage. For a minute, Mary just watched him, watched his hair blowing in the wind along with the bottom of his jacket.

She could see from the window that his body was still. Dead still. There was no breathing; his back did not lift up and lower back down from his lungs, taking in air and releasing it. She did sense a pulse from the body though, and that was enough to snap her out of the momentary shock she was in. Mary broke into a full sprint to the door and burst outside so hard, the door hinges nearly came loose.

Upon making it to Dale's body, she flipped him over effortlessly and lifted his head—laying it on her legs. "What happened, Dale? Who did this to you? Talk to me, please." She knew that she sensed a pulse, and she was right. Dale's eyes were open. He blinked rapidly, trying to fight death from overcoming him, trying to speak. His blood-covered lips quivered as they parted, showing pink teeth. He was a long way from being able to speak words. Mary observed him while rubbing her hands through his hair, trying to comfort him.

Glub, glub was the only sound coming from his mouth. Or throat— she wasn't sure which. *Glub, glub,* he said, eyes blinking faster than she'd ever seen before. The look on his face seemed to say he was drowning. His veins were bulging from his forehead, and his eyes were nearly oozing from his face, threatening to pop out. *Glub. Glub. Glub.*

Mary noticed the front of his shirt was torn open, in small slices— slices that open wounds showed through. "Who did this, Dale?"

He'd been stabbed in the stomach. The pants he wore were covered in blood. An artery or major organ had been hit by the knife, she knew it. Mary put her hand over the wound and tried her best to keep the blood inside. Her idea did nothing to stop it. It was too late for him. Without someone around that could do surgery, he would die. Marcella was a long way from where they were, and she was likely dead now.

Well yeah, you left her. You left them all to die, Sirus said. "Shut up! Just leave me alone!" Mary screamed aloud. Just as she noticed that

71

she was screaming at a voice that only existed in her mind, she saw them.

There were three men walking from between two houses, across the street from where she lay in the driveway with Dale. The men did not run at her, nor did they look wary of her. They thought she was an easy mark, and she just knew they were the "come with us...or else" type of men. All three were gigantic compared to her. The thought of them ganging up on Dale, slaughtering him the way they did, ignited her fire inside. What was normally a tiny ember barely alight in her gut now began to smolder, and burn hotter. She knew that if she could get rid of those guys fast enough, then maybe she could try surgery herself.

She wanted to hurt them badly. Not only for Dale, but...simply because it would please her to do so. Mary freed her legs by pushing Dale's body to the cement with no regard for him. Yes, she wanted to help him, but at the moment, nothing was more important than inflicting pain and death...the deaths of those who saw her as easy work. As they made their way to the road only twenty or so yards from her, their faces had arrogance written all over them. Mary was so overjoyed that she bit her lip hard enough for it to bleed. She stood up and untucked the long white shirt she'd found in the bedroom of the house, where two others now lay awaiting the decomposition process.

The long white shirt, which no doubt had belonged to the father, moved wildly behind her the same way her long dark hair did. She began walking toward the three soldiers, who all had weapons. She had none, and she needed none. But...just as she picked up speed in her stride, the dull metal object that had once taken down a massive ship reacted to her bloodlust, her desperation, and her hunger to hurt. Maybe she did have a weapon.

With one hand, Mary reached into her pocket to grab the metal object. Her other hand suddenly became engulfed in that beautiful multi-colored flame as she lifted it into the sky. Mary's eyes became darker, just as the clouds above became darker.

The sun retreated behind the clouds. Rumbling could be heard in the distance as streaks of light crackled through and around the darkened clouds. What was once arrogance and pretension now became fear and terror. They were not normal men though; they wouldn't run away from her. Instead, the men pulled their triggers, firing off round after round...to no avail. She was no longer in front of them—and she was able to assume they no longer believed her an easy mark.

15

DAVID

"I wanted to speak with you particularly, only you. I know that you have always worked closely with Sirus on parts of this experiment. No one else here would know his ways as much as you do." David was not huge on smiling or playing around subjects. He stared at Teacher Simon from the same seat Sirus would walk laps around and study his specimens from as he lied to them about getting into the Greater Understanding Program, only to have Teacher Simon eliminate them shortly after.

"I do know him well. I couldn't imagine that I could tell you anything about him the Order doesn't already know." Simon sat in the visitor seat across the massive oak desk. The same seat that Old World members would sit in while being played with like the toys they were, then shuffled out into the hallway where he would be waiting for them.

"Don't tell me what you could and couldn't imagine. I'm not here to ask your opinion on anything. Answer my questions and spare me the small talk. Please do not mistake me for Sirus; I have no qualms with pushing my rank to have this entire experiment deleted and everyone repurposed to other places. Including you." Again, there was no smile, no change in reaction at all. Everything David said came out in a voice that was monotone, stale, and uncaring. His tone made him sound as if he spent his days squashing the plans of others.

"I understand, sir. How can I be of service to you?" Teacher Simon said, massaging the tips of his fingers into the desk—as was typical for him.

"Now that we understand each other, let's keep these meetings very short. Besides all the nonsense littering the office," David lifted a hand from his lap, gesturing at the Old World objects around the room, "is there anything else that Sirus liked to keep around? Something out of the ordinary?"

"I don't think I comprehend what you are asking me, sir. I do not have any information on anything like that. I knew this office held novelties that meant something to him, but I didn't think that was out of protocol for this exercise. The only specimens to see those pieces were on their way to being eliminated anyway," Teacher Simon said.

"No, the nonsensical accessories he is so attached to in this room are not out of protocol at all. While they are self-serving and unnecessary, we do not mind him having his attachments to the features his research created. I'm more interested in…weaponry he may have been attached to from our own star system, from OUR home." David placed both his hands palms up in front of him, then moved them toward Teacher Simon and back to himself. "Do you have any knowledge of Sirus having anything from our home, here in this reality?"

"No sir. If I had any information on such a thing, I would have alerted you or one of the others."

"I've had men search this Palace, and I'll have more search every one of these facilities you both had set up. I don't know why, but something tells me that you aren't being honest with me." David's eyes zeroed in on Teacher Simon. The look made the teacher jump just a bit. "Would you like to know why I don't think you are being straightforward? I'll tell you."

"I assure you, sir…" Teacher Simon lifted his long bony hands from the desk. The lit candles on the right side of the desk created the illusion that he had only half a face, the dark shadows in the office casting an ominous glow over everything.

"I'm talking," David said, unbothered by the elevated tone and reaction of the teacher sitting across from him. "I know that you aren't being honest with me because when I asked about Sirus having something else here with him, you pretended you knew nothing at all. In order for me to believe that, Simon, I'd have to believe that you have not lived for countless years—I'd have to believe your deduction skills are lacking. In a position like this…if I were to believe that about you, well, we would need to get rid you of."

Teacher Simon's already large oval-shaped eyes grew exponentially after hearing those words. "Please, David. I did not intend to—"

David cut the teacher off mid-sentence. "If I have to remind you of your place one more time…let's just say you won't like what happens next. Allow me to make my point. Then I'll let you tell another lie," David said, watching Teacher Simon's body seem to deflate with disappointment. It looked more like the teacher was powering down as his head and shoulders slowly lowered.

"Yes, sir."

"You knew about Sirus's manifestation link being blown up. I know that you know because every specimen in the Palace knows. Now, if you did know about that ship being destroyed, you would also immediately know how that happened. There is only one way to harm a manifestation link in this reality. Never mind why Sirus would find it necessary to call upon such a thing to deal with his own creations, my point still stands. You know how that event happens." David spun the golden globe on the desk while speaking, choosing not to make eye contact with the teacher across from him.

"Only a Lohar stone could do such a thing, Simon. I know that, and you know that. So, the question becomes: How did a stone like that even get to this planet, or even in this reality sector? I'd think the maker would be responsible for that, especially a creator that has a history of self-praise and a flare for theatrics."

Teacher Simon did not respond. He gazed up to the ceiling, which was covered with an artistic painting of some specimen from the past. He shook his head but said nothing. The warning had been made.

"Since I've arrived back to this silly place, it's been a mystery to me,

I must admit. My own mind tells me that the stones, one of which we did retrieve from the battlefield, materialized here for a specific purpose—and that purpose was not to have his own ship destroyed. Sirus nearly lost his life, which spans eons a million times over. While he has always been a wildcard to the Order, he is a masterful creator and would not bring something that could undo himself...without a purpose. I have an idea what purpose he had in mind, but I'm going to wait until specific information comes back on that theory."

Teacher Simon no longer looked like himself. The being that had carried out countless killings and a slew of other missions for the program director over millions of years, in one form or another, was no longer his stoic, unmoved, and cold self. One could even say he became more human in that moment, if only for a moment.

What was to be believed when it came to Teacher Simon, the man of many faces and aliases? He slumped down in his seat, in fear... mortal fear, because while their people were not human, they were not immortal either. David could and would cause him many manners of harm—or the unthinkable.

Teacher Simon reluctantly raised his right hand, directing his attention back to David from the ceiling. "May I say my piece on this subject, sir?" His voice shook and trembled like rolling thunder behind a massive mountain range creeping into the forefront. David heard the fear, and he enjoyed it. He'd always enjoyed such things, but this was the way of their people. While being highly intelligent, the Lohar beings were a warring people secondarily. What moved them, gave them life and happiness, was expansion, creation, and war.

While the Palace program was and had always been a creation of Sirus's, a "pet project," David had always thought of it as nothing more than this. Outside of the different experiments and tests, the Lohar had been and always would be expanding throughout unknown spaces and times. Their people had existed this way even before the Big Bang that created the universe of the program David found himself overseeing all of a sudden.

"Yes Simon, you may now speak."

"I...I just want to reiterate and hold firm on my word that if Sirus had plans outside of the normal procedures regarding this program, I know nothing about them. While I have worked under him for a time, my allegiance belongs to the Order, and the Lohar. Always has and always will. I will do anything that I can in order to help you get to the bottom of this situation." Teacher Simon produced the words as fast as he could.

The corner of David's mouth turned up in a slight grin, not quite, but as close to a smile as he could manage at that time. "Funny that you say you will help out, because that's what I've mostly called you here for. I need something taken care of—something of the utmost importance if we are to finalize this exercise and move on. Of course, I'll have to have your mind synced to make sure you don't know anything...harmful. But if you pass those tests with flying colors, we will move forward.

"Be calm, Simon. I'm speaking to every teacher, watcher, and security agent in the Palace. It's not personal, but I must and will get to the bottom of this situation. I hope you understand that." David rolled the chair back from the desk and stood. Without offering his hand, only gazing at the door, he waved a hand and dismissed Teacher Simon from the office.

1 6

TEACHER SIMON

MAKING IT BACK TO HIS ROOM IN THE BASEMENT OF THE PALACE, SIMON thought to himself about what David had said. He wondered if his fear was believable to the man now in charge of the Palace program—or what was left of it anyway. He carefully weaved his way past the many instruments that inhabited the space he called home...for now. He longed for his real home, but for now, where he was would suffice. Simon sat down in the lone chair in the back right corner of his pristine white room.

For a long time, he'd been good at deception. After all, it was his job to do this on Sirus's behalf. As with any man or being, jobs could become cumbersome, and doing the same thing time after time would eventually lose its luster. The wandering mind was a dangerous thing, especially after it became eroded from the machinations of different outcomes and possibilities.

Simon stretched his abnormally long legs out as far as they would go, while doing the same with his arms. He sat like that in the chair, resembling an oversized cross more than a man in that moment. Taking in a deep breath and releasing it slowly, allowing his body to relax, Simon pulled his limbs back in as he took on the form of *The Thinker* statue.

Simon recalled the statue by Auguste Rodin, first created as a part of his works in the group titled *The Gates of Hell*. The pose was of a man sitting with one elbow on his knee, his chin resting on his hand. The man was in deep thought as he was surrounded by a perceived hell.

Simon sat there, plotting out the next few parts of his plan, always needing to stay a few steps ahead. He thought that what he had set into motion, ending Sirus's time within that reality (at least for now) was for the best. A long time coming even. Some from Lohar thought the Earth experiment had gone much longer than it should have. Expediting the results were best for everyone involved as far as he was concerned.

There is no reason why I should tell David or anyone how the Lohar weapons found their way into this world. No reason to tell them I planted them. The less his superiors knew, the less work he needed to do, meaning he could get back to his home and move on to other realities that served his…talents and ambitions much better.

David was a trifling being with no foresight for what was possible in the different realities he and Sirus had created over the time stream. He saw them as silly games and a waste of time. He didn't say so, but Simon could hear it in his tone. Many from their home world did not view the experiments created by him and his predecessor with the same vigor as other options available in Lohar. Many thought their reality streams and time warps were nothing more than games, childish games to pass time. They were wrong though, very wrong, and he would show them the error of those thoughts.

Even Sirus had not seen the scope of what they had created. Of course, the Earth exercise was a lost cause. Sirus implanted himself into the world far too often, and he was always the scapegoat to create that push and pull the humans needed to sleep at night. Without Simon constantly being the other side of the coin, the versions of Earth would have plummeted a lot faster than they did.

Simon took his hand away from his chin. He placed the palms of both hands on his knees and began massaging the tips of his fingers into the material of his pants. Doing that helped Simon focus even more on what those around him planned. He knew that the boy Lonnie had ambitions of becoming the "god of the New World." Simon said the phrase aloud, but quietly. How silly of him, but it made sense. There would need to be someone in charge when he and his kind returned to whence they came.

That person would not be Lonnie of course, but the thought was courageous, he would give the young man that. Simon had a deep and quiet dislike for humankind. Not because of anything they did, but because of what they reflected. They were prideful, self-serving at all times, and overly impressed with themselves. Much like the man who was responsible for losing his manifestation link.

Humankind could not and would not prosper because they were too much like Sirus...and that's the way Sirus wanted it. In order for the program to be successful, Simon needed to find a way to eliminate Sirus for a while and get the higher-ups into the picture. Those who wore the yellow coats were clearly not happy with what was going on, and they would surely report to those who were not to be spoken of. One day Simon hoped that Sirus would forgive him. They would speak again, he was sure of it, just not within the current reality. Not if he was able to get things finalized before the Palace director found a way back inside.

Simon stood up from the seat. He moved around the room full of instruments, strumming the harp here, tapping a drum there, still deep in thought. Most of what he did had to do with thinking deeply and plotting what would come next. It was always about what came next; being progressive and ahead of the game was key to him.

Even before the most recent sickness came to wipe out most of their specimens, he was plotting this moment. There was a young woman Simon used to plant the two Lohar weapons in the perfect spot, knowing that that all things involved would come to past and that the very Palace on those grounds would be taken over at some point.

A rare smile materialized on Simon's face. His plan had worked, as his plans always did. A little too well, but it did work. Mary now had one of those weapons and the means to use it, but she had no understanding of how to use it on command, nor was it in her nature to ever get to that point.

Simon picked up a flute and placed his fingers accordingly to make the sweetest sound that anyone could have ever heard. A sound so pure and beautiful that it threatened to drive a person mad. He played only one tone and moved on, making his way through the other instruments lined up in rows around the room—touching them, strumming them, and blowing into different wind instruments as he went.

After a time, the room sounded like a full symphony was at work. Even when he was done using each instrument, it continued the sound he'd produced. Music was Simon's favorite thing, and just like everything else, it would bend to his will. Lonnie would march to the sound of his drum, and so would Mary. They were but mere small pieces on a massive board to be rearranged in the ways he saw fit.

For the rest of the night Simon moved around the room, listening to the sounds of his own creation. Thinking, planning, plotting...

This was his way.

17

MARY

WHEN THERE WAS THE TIME FOR MORE KILLING, THERE WOULD ALSO BE
the time to dig graves. Digging the graves of those you cared for, those
you cared for and fought alongside. Mary found herself digging a
grave for Dale, who'd only been away from his squad for a full day.
Now he lay in the driveway of a vacant home, bleeding out on the
spotless driveway. His blood created a trail from the deep wounds in
his back all the way down to the curb, then wherever that curb led to.

She stood in the backyard of the home alone, holding a dirty spade
she'd found leaning up against the side of the house. The flame that
appeared around her hand when she'd entered "the dark place," as
she'd begun calling it, had long since gone out. Now her hand was just
as soft and lukewarm as it was the day she was born. Mary stared into
the sky and thought about what life was for humans outside of the
Palace, and a part of her began to wonder if life wasn't in fact better
for them inside. The Order's games and all. She knew that the end
game was to get rid of Old World members eventually, but was having
twenty-plus years of what some might call happiness before being
forced from existence not better than what waited for them in the
broken world outside?

She propped her foot on the top of the spade. Sweat poured from her brow as she flipped her long hair to the side, and she noticed that she was sweating more digging the grave for Dale than when she'd killed the men who had brought him death. Killing was easy, effortless for her—doing the work of "caring" was not so much. That type of work had only brought her heartache and tears.

Mary set her aim back to the hole in the ground she'd been digging. It was not quite six feet, but it was deep enough to give Dale a decent burial without fear of animals getting to him in the dead of the night. One last clump of dirt to the side and she'd be done. Surprisingly, she did not cry after the fight with the three men. She expected that Dale would die; she was no doctor, and he was already dying from the wound and infection growing in his shoulder. Most likely they did him a service by sending him out a bit early and saving him some terrible nights of pain before the inevitable happened.

You don't cry anymore because you are learning...it doesn't matter, Mary. Death is normal, and natural. Only power gives meaning, and I created you with tons of it. The voice tickling the back of her mind spoke in a matter-of-fact manner, trailing off at the end. Mary decided to stop pushing the voice away when it came to her—doing so rarely worked anyway. She'd let him say what he wanted to, and in the end, it was up to her to be influenced or not. She did wonder if that meant he had truly gone somewhere else, or if he was now living in her mind through some link she'd created when she destroyed the monstrous ship.

That couldn't be the case though. She'd used the very same weapon to aid in the killing of the three men, and she didn't hear their words echoing inside her mind. Mary flung the last bit of dirt into the pile she'd been accumulating to her right. That was enough. She tossed the shovel on top of the pile of dirt and headed back to the front yard to retrieve Dale. The hole was sizeable enough for one. She didn't bother to create burial plots for the other men, or those inside the house. Night predators could carry them off into the woods and feed themselves for days, weeks, months—she didn't care.

Grasping Dale's hands, she dragged his body to the backyard. She could lift him if she had to, but the dead weight would be a lot for her to carry, especially when the fire was not burning inside her. Being in battle, moving at blinding speeds, and the amazing strength and focus it took to shoot so accurately did require a lot of stamina. Fighting, regardless of how long or short, would leave her exhausted afterwards.

Having the option to be ready for a fight if more Palace-born members jumped on her was necessary, and she feared that would be impossible if she carried the dead man on her shoulder. She was sure he wouldn't mind the way she'd dragged him.

While dragging the man who'd been fighting alongside her just the day before, her mind returned to the state of what was going on out there. How long had life been that way? Based on what she knew of the Old World, they'd always been like that. Killing, hurting, capturing life for the sake of it. Only humans seemed to kill each other simply for sport—Mary could not think of any other lifeform that would concern themselves with such a self-destructive action. Humans were prone to it, and at all times. Not that she was any different...maybe she was worse. The thought pained her deeply. *But, are you even human?* she wondered. Of course she was, but more.

How much more? a voice echoed deep from within.

The question that had been wading in the deep end of her mind came back to her in moments of self-reflection concerning the state of everyone around her. How was she different? She was doing the same things they were doing, and with much higher efficiency. Sirus had told her what she needed to know about herself twice already in person. Once in his office when Jacob was with her, and again on the field with the rebel squad present. The voice in her mind could not be trusted; it was an annoyance at best. Mary knew that visually she was a human. She even felt like a human, as far as she could tell from her own feelings in comparison to how the others felt.

Look, you are even beginning to separate yourself from the lower level creations. "The others," you said. I like that. It's true and you know it. You are more, Sirus spoke again.

By the time she delivered Dale's body to the hole she'd dug for him, she was pouring sweat again. Caring about people was hard work, she was beginning to see that. Since escaping the Palace, this was the first time she'd been traveling around the world on her own. The thought felt selfish but refreshing at the same time. She would no longer feel the need to listen to what someone else thought (she wasn't counting the voice of the program director) or deal with them slowing her down. Much could be done alone with her abilities and the weapons procured from the Palace-born soldiers.

The object in her pocket was even becoming a help, and the way to use its power was becoming apparent to her. She still did not know how to call upon the power at will, but—the fact that she had been able to do it again told her that it did work. After burying Dale, she planned on self-examining her mental state in both instances of use. Mary knew enough to know that with the weapon, she could end the Order's stranglehold on the area. There was the thought of why they hadn't used such weapons against her or the rebel Palace long ago. The weapon was most definitely from wherever they were from, Sirus had said so himself. He had called it a weapon of the Lo...Lo...Loher... or Lohar. Something like that. There were two; she could only guess that they'd picked up the one that Logan had.

Mary decided to push the thoughts of battle and humankind away for the moment while she spoke some words to her friend's body. She didn't know why it felt important to do such a thing, but it did. She sat next to Dale's body there in the grass, next to the crypt she'd dug for the young man.

"I'm sorry that you've become caught up in all of this." Mary placed a hand on Dale's cheek, wiping away dirt and grime. He seemed to be at peace, almost as if he were asleep. In a way he was, a final sleep of sorts. "I know that what happened to your squad and the Palace you all worked so hard to take over was mainly my fault. Simply being there put you in danger, even more danger than what you'd been accustomed to." Her voice was calm. She spoke to Dale as if he were there listening to her.

"There is not much that I can say to you, Dale, except that I cared for you as much as a person could in the small time we had together. Not in the exact same way that I cared for another"—Jacob's face popped into her mind then—"but you were the most special of any member in the squad. There was a connection, I think." Mary stopped speaking and pondered that thought. She was no longer capable of feeling the way she once felt for Jacob.

That feeling had been gunned down on a different field some time ago, back when she was with child and the man that meant more than being alive was running with her to what they thought would be the rest of their lives. Had he lived, they would have eventually run into that Eagle squad together, and Jacob would have been reunited with his childhood best friend. Mary smiled at the thought.

"I have a promise I want to make to you. Not only to you, but to all the members of the Eagle squad. If you are somewhere with them now, please relay this message. I will make this right. I will avenge their deaths, but not just theirs…I'll avenge what happened to your world. A world that doesn't belong to me or the Palace-born people… this was your planet, and it was taken away. That debt will be paid by my hand. That's my promise."

Mary could hear a small whisper from a place deep within saying: *It was never theirs. It was always mine and mine alone to decide upon the course ahead. And, even further than that.* She'd expected him to say as much, but even still, they didn't deserve what happened to them. She had the ability to bring some type of justification to their loss, and so she would. This was now her life's motivation. There was nothing else —no love, no child, nothing more to look forward to. She didn't know everything, but she knew enough to get along on her own.

Mary lowered her face to give Dale a kiss on the cheek. "I'm gonna get going. I need to find a safe place to think about my next move. This is goodbye. I hope that you live somewhere else out there, I hope you all d—"

Just then, the sound of sticks snapping came from the northern part of the backyard. It was the sound of a boot stepping down; she knew that. The continuous slow burn inside of her ratcheted up to a flame in that moment. Immediately, Mary pushed her friend's body into the hole and vaulted to her feet—covering the twenty yards of the backyard to make it to where the sound had come from. The speed with which she moved made her look like a blur, a wicked wraith with silky hair flying across twenty yards in a second. She was taking steps, but they were so fast that the human eye could not pick them up before it was too late.

This was the case for who was spying on her. And it was already too late. Before he knew that she even noticed him, she was there in his face with the blade of her knife scraping against the skin on his throat. The man, or young man, screamed out, "Please, please don't kill me!"

"Why shouldn't I? You were trying to get the drop on me. Why were you watching me?" Mary spoke in a whisper with her face pressed to the side of his so that she could speak directly into his ear, the knife still pressed against his neck.

"I'm sorry, I'm sorry...I don't mean any harm. I just wanted to see you. To see for myself. Here, take my gun." The young man's hand slowly moved to his hip.

"Don't do that." Mary's free hand grabbed his and forced it against his body. "Who are you, and what do you want with me?"

"I'm—I'm Branden," he stuttered. She could feel him trying to control his movements—he clearly knew enough about her to know that she would kill him for the slightest movement. The young man took a deep breath, then spoke once more. "I just want to give you some information I recovered from one of those soldiers near that big building." He nodded in the direction of the rebel Palace.

PART II

IT'S IN THE EYES

18

LONNIE

"How's that even possible?" Lonnie slammed his hand down on the table hard enough to knock his cup of coffee to the ground. He could have caught the cup before it toppled over, but opted not to. He was pissed and didn't care that the cleaners would have extra work in his pod that day. "I sent my two best!" he yelled.

"Not only did she dispatch both of them in less than two minutes apart from each other—I sent three of the top gunners from a different Palace in the area as backup. They are also dead," Teacher Simon said, standing next to the table and chairs in Lonnie's pod. His hands were clasped behind his back as he stood straight, delivering the info to the Palace captain.

"How could you know they are all dead? You aren't out there. If no one made it back, how could you know? I don't believe you." Lonnie averted his gaze, his eyes darting around the room, not looking at anything in particular. His brain was winding, thinking of possibilities that would make this news untrue or unreliable.

"We have our ways of knowing when one of the soldiers go offline, and this is the case. There are no mistakes to be made in these cases. They are all dead...period. If you need more convincing, I can bring you to the...higher-ups." The teacher no longer scared Lonnie, and he even gave Lonnie the respect that was due to someone of his stature in the Palace. But it was also clear that the man did not take kindly to the idea that the Order didn't know what was going on with their operatives.

Lonnie sneered at the giant of a man, then looked away again before getting to his feet, leaving the teacher there at the table and moving to the closet. He ripped a shirt off a hanger, snapping the plastic in the process. Lonnie pulled the gray shirt with the "Just do it" logo over his head—slamming the closet door afterwards.

"Don't fret, sir. I have a plan. We have a plan, and it involves you and me working more closely together," Teacher Simon said without turning to look at Lonnie. Still, he stood in the same position with his hands behind him.

Lonnie began walking toward Teacher Simon. "What makes you think I'd want to work with you in this matter? It's my job to find Mary and bring her back, and I'll do so on my own. I will have no one taking the credit for what I must do."

Teacher Simon turned to Lonnie just as he stopped inches away from the teacher's face, or chest. While Lonnie was tall himself, standing at six-two, the teacher dwarfed him, standing no less than six-nine. Teacher Simon gazed down on Lonnie in confusion. Lonnie didn't know how to read the thoughts going on behind his large eyes. Simon's dark eyes blinked slowly, regarding him in a way that made Lonnie feel researched or observed.

"I will say this one time, and only one time. I fear that you are forgetting your role. We all have roles to play in this, as well as outside of this situation." Teacher Simon's dead pupils dilated, giving him the look of a mask. Lonnie could sense no life in his face, no emotion. He'd never noticed the man's eyes quite like he did at that moment. He couldn't show it, but he was afraid to move, to speak, or to think the wrong thing out of fear that the teacher would do something terrible to him. Something worse than death.

"Watch your tone with me, Lonnie. I'm here to help you in your goals and aspirations. However lofty those may be. You have won your respect from me, but continuing to press the issue with aggression and a sharp tongue will put you in the same place where I've put more..." Teacher Simon blinked, only one time, then he continued to speak, "...souls than you can possibly fathom with your feeble mind. I know how much you know of who we are, and I know that your brain is moving on all cylinders. A level of genius for your kind would still only be able to understand a tenth of a percent of what we are."

At no point during his speaking did the teacher ever unclasp his hands from behind his back. Lonnie believed that he didn't need to in order to stop any kind of attack if it were to happen. He didn't know how he knew that...*But it's in the eyes*, he thought. *The man could do unspeakable mental damage to me simply with those eyes.* Lonnie felt his legs involuntarily take a step back.

"We will be working together. That's the case, and I'd like that relationship to go easily. And I hope that we can see your goals be realized. Allow me to help you without the childish comments and attitude. I can do the mission without you, but for the sake of Sirus's program, I'd rather have you there to get training and receive the credit. I have no use for such things. That is what we put you in this position for, after all, to learn and move up. Don't talk yourself out of position, Lonnie," Teacher Simon said.

"Yes...yes, sir. I do understand." Lonnie wanted nothing more in that moment than for the man known as Teacher Simon to be out of his pod. "We should...work together, sir. Whatever you say, I'll do that."

The teacher's pupils seemed to flash like a shutter on a camera. And just like that, he was back to normal, or as normal as the giant man could be. Lonnie had no idea what those eyes were doing, but he didn't like it. While speaking to Simon, it felt like they were alone in the dark, like there was only darkness and a million sets of those big wandering, scanning eyes watching him. The isolation and nakedness of the experience made the hairs on the back of his neck stand up.

"Good. Trust me, it's in your best interest if you want what you say you do." Teacher Simon walked past him and over to the couch. He sat down. "Sit. Let's speak like teammates, and not bother with idea of rankings and roles. That time is over. We have the same goal—it's time we realize that goal on our own. The job is for us, not others whom we can send. None can stop her but us. That is clear."

Lonnie hesitantly walked to the couch, where Teacher Simon was looking as awkward as the man always did whenever his long legs folded to sit. He sat down next to the teacher, and they talked.

MARY

THEY SAT TOGETHER IN THE BACKYARD NEXT TO THE NOW COVERED hole she'd dug for her friend. The man named Branden, who must have been a few years younger than her, helped cover the hole and made a headstone of two sticks crossed over each other as a marker. Branden stuck the marker into the dirt of the grave. Mary had no idea why he did that part—but it did look better that way, so she allowed it.

It took all the convincing Branden could muster to get Mary to let him go without slicing his throat open and leaving his body there in the same wooded area he'd been spying on her from. He said he'd been deciding how he would approach her—but it still felt like spying to her. In the end, he had convinced her that he meant no harm and did want to relay information to her.

"Thank you for believing me...Mary. You are Mary, correct?" he said.

"A little too late for that question, don't you think? You've just helped me bury a body." Mary stared at him, wondering what he could possibly have to tell her about her own people. He laughed at her comment, swiping his hair away from his eyes and rubbing sweat from his brow as he nervously picked grass from the ground.

"Yeah, yeah...I guess you are right." Branden caught Mary's intense gaze, meeting her eyes with his. "All of those soldier guys at that massive building not too far from here are looking for you. I can see from the bodies in the street around the front of the house, and your friend here, that you already know that. But—"

Mary cut in. "Right, I do know that. First, let me ask you something. How did you come by your information to begin with?"

A grin transformed his face. Making him appear older, wiser, and a tad demented. "I caught the guy," Branden said, shrugging his shoulders like it was no big deal.

"Define 'caught him,'" Mary said with disbelief creeping into her tone. If what he said was true, she'd possibly stumbled upon someone who could help her in what was to come. Not so much that he'd get in the way, but still, it was good to have at least one ally. With her right hand, she rubbed the pocket of her pants where the weapon was. The mysterious object was a very good friend to have as well. It was unreliable as hell at this point, but still a game changer.

"Like, I subdued him, knocked him out, then I used my rope to tie him to a tree...and made him tell me what I wanted to know. I didn't know you, obviously, but he was very forthcoming with information. I was mostly interested in the battle that had taken place there, what with all the dead bodies, and, oh yeah—the huge metal ship thing that could be seen falling from the sky from miles away." As he spoke the last sentence, Branden's eyes widened and his brows lifted. His surprised face matched the high pitch of his voice.

Mary ignored the part about the destroyed flying ship and the dead bodies, knowing that getting into the conversation would only serve to make her furious. Lots of those dead bodies belonged to her people. "Hmm, if you were able to disarm and kidnap a Palace soldier, then you must have some decent combat skills," Mary said softly, quietly impressed with what the young man did.

"I guess you could say so. I learned a few things here and there. Not much else to do in this gigantic crazy world." He lifted his hands to the sky, smiling.

"Learned from who though? Are you part of another rebel group? I was told that the Eagle squad was not the only one."

Branden pulled more grass from the dirt, tossing it around nonchalantly. The lighthearted smile on his face dissolved into something that looked like embarrassment mixed with shame. "Nah, my mother taught me a lot about hunting. My father handled the combat training. Not because they were a violent people—they were far from that—but just in case...in case the men in the white vans ever found us."

He pulled up a plug of grass and dirt, chucking it over his shoulder. The clump of earth banged against the side of the house. Branden returned to pulling blades of grass up and swatting at flying insects. Mary could see that talking about his parents made him unhappy, or at least uncomfortable.

"Did the men in the white vans ever find you all? Are your parents close to here?" Mary asked.

"Yes and no." Branden looked away.

"I'm sorry, Branden. If I said something that caused you to become offended, that was not my intention," Mary said, being sure not to change her tone. She meant no offense, but at the same time, she needed to know or understand how someone like him could subdue a Palace soldier and walk away unscathed.

He peered back at her, his eyes now red and glassy. "Long story as short as I can possibly make it. Here it is. I'm not really sure why I'm telling you this, but I see no reason not to, and I already know a bunch about you, so...fair is fair.

"It was always me, Mom, and Dad. Until one day, the men in the white vans actually did get out of their vehicles and came into the neighborhood we were living in. Something they'd never done before, they chose to do on a day where I was out, fucking off playing ball by myself."

"Was there anyone else in the neighborhood?" Mary said.

"No, everyone is dead, as you know. I mean, yeah, there are some still alive, but they aren't behaving like normal people. They are either out killing each other for scraps, or banding together into mob groups to take on the guys in the white vans. Just listen though. It's hard for me to talk about it. I'd like to get everything out, then you can ask me questions. Fair?" Branden was speaking fast.

"Fair." Mary nodded.

"Okay, thank you." Branden looked away again, out at the sky beyond the metal fence enclosing the backyard. "I came home to find my mother dead on the kitchen floor, and my father dead in his study. There were three men there. I was too shocked to even think of fighting back...at that moment.

"Once they put me in the car, my brain switched to survival mode. Then the skills I'd been taught came in handy. I disarmed the man in the back with me, grabbed his gun, and killed all three guys." Branden faced Mary again. A single tear rolled own his cheek. It didn't get far before he quickly wiped it away. "That was some time ago though. I don't even know how long. A year, maybe two." He forced a sad smile.

"Ever since then, I've never stopped moving. Now I travel around this area, tracking and hunting the men in the vans. I want to make sure they never get to take everything away from someone else...like they did me. I'm a hunter—those are the skills I used to catch and tie up the guy who gave me information. The same information I'm trying to tell you now." He giggled. That time it was authentic, and she giggled right along with him.

"Okay, okay...I'm sorry you had to relive that moment, but now I can better understand how you did what you claimed to do. Now, you may tell me what you know."

20

LONNIE

"Mary is different from you, or the other soldiers we have here." Teacher Simon sat there on the couch, his long arm stretching behind Lonnie along the length of the small sofa. His knees were high as they bent in his weird sitting position. Whenever the teacher sat down, Lonnie would think about how his build wasn't made for anything but standing. To him, it was funny and terrifying at the same time. He'd seen tall men before, that wasn't the issue—but this man was more than tall. His build appeared and felt different. It seemed a labor for Simon to accomplish the simple act of sitting.

"Okay, in what way do you mean different? I don't understand. What's so different about Mary?" Lonnie asked.

"If you were out on the battlefield with her, I'm sure you saw or heard of her tactical prowess. I'm sure you saw the ship come crashing down to the Earth below. That was all her. Now, while you and the other soldiers are a step beyond any Old World members in the way of combat, thinking, and tactics—Mary is a step or two above you." The teacher spoke without looking directly at Lonnie, his eyes focused on the TV screen in the wall in front of them.

Lonnie knew he paid no attention to what was being broadcasted, which was more Old World clips of atrocities they'd done to the planet before the sickness. The current video on the screen showed men dumping toxic waste into one of the oceans. The humans of old were a self-destructive people, if nothing else.

"The reason behind her difference is not so easy to answer. I'm not necessarily authorized to give that info. Even to a high-ranking captain like yourself. That information would need to come directly from the program director. And, as you know, I'm sure he is incapacitated."

Lonnie moved uncomfortably on the sofa, adjusting his weight and trying not to look pissed off at what was being said. "With all due respect, Teacher Simon, I would need to know information like this in order to catch her, in order to know her, in order to protect my men against her. We prepared for the battle thinking we were on equal ground with everyone in that Palace, and now I'm finding out that wasn't the case at all?" Lonnie spoke to the side of Teacher Simon's bald head as the man stared straight ahead.

"I understand how you feel, as I said—the information must come from the Palace program director. And if he didn't see fit to give you the information, he didn't think it was need-to-know. It's not my place to go into any further detail outside of what I'm telling you now. You need not worry about putting the soldiers you lead into harm's way concerning Mary anymore. We are going in a different direction as far as Mary." Teacher Simon began kneading his fingers into the surface of the sofa. One hand working away on the back of the couch, and the other on the right arm of the couch.

"Okay, so basically the gist of this is that Mary is more combat-inclined than myself and my men. I get it. I'd like to understand why, but I'm sure I'll find out at some point. What do we do? How do we stop her?" Lonnie could feel himself beginning to lose his calm. The sooner he was able to wrangle up the girl, the sooner he could begin to realize his goal: ingratiating himself to the members of the Order who were making the important decisions. One single woman should not be that hard to stop. Sure, she was strong, but he had an army and backup from multiple Palaces in the area.

In his mind, he knew that he was being viewed as weak, as if he could not capture the woman on his own and now needed help from one of the teachers. That made him inflamed. And now he was learning that Mary was even more special than he once thought. Lonnie recalled her movements on the field that day. The speed, dexterity, and aim were all off the charts. He saw it with his own eyes, and it didn't scare him. He wanted to get close enough to engage with her, but that chance had been taken away from him when her people grabbed her—pushing her back inside the Palace. He would have his time with her though, he knew that.

"Well, you and I will go after her together. Just us, no one else. You have great tracking skills, and I have a unique set of abilities. While I'm not trained for war or battles, I am suited for a more personal approach, and against someone like Mary—that's what we will need," Teacher Simon said.

Lonnie figured something like that was coming, and while he did not disagree with the approach, he wanted to make sure that one hundred percent of the credit belonged to him. He could not have the teacher helping too much and muddying his hard work. "Okay, I think this is a great plan. When do we leave?"

Teacher Simon finally turned his head to look at Lonnie. "We will leave in the A.M. I'll come to collect you once all the intel is in place. Be prepared." One hard blink, and then the teacher awkwardly stood up. Still, the image made Lonnie tense. He didn't know why he'd never noticed the large, almost bulb-shaped eyes of Simon. They now seemed to be alive, working independently of the man entirely.

"I'll be ready. See you then."

21

AMY

"But what do we do now?" she said to Mark, wondering if he was strong enough to deal with the fallout of their decisions. He looked confused, afraid, and ready to crawl into a shell if there was one around. "Mark!" she screamed at him. The man jumped, spinning around to face her.

"I don't know! I don't know, Amy! We didn't quite plan this part out. You know that—you tell me what comes next." Mark was becoming unhinged. She supposed that was normal for what they'd all just seen and took part in. Caused even. There was no time for that right now though; there would be people looking at them for guidance, wanting to know what was to come next. And the two people who should be the most confident could not be seen arguing and screaming back and forth at each other.

"Listen, Mark, keep your voice down. There are tons of people out there waiting on us, wanting to know what we should do next. We can't go out on that stage with no plan in mind. I get it, man, I really do. We barely believed this would all work to begin with, and now that it has, we don't know exactly what to do. But let's talk it out as quickly as we can. They are waiting."

In the auditorium of Palace 478 sat three hundred and eighty-nine people. Some Old World members and some Palace-born. There was not one teacher to be found, no watchers, and no security guards, for they were all gone. What was once called Albany, NY a long time ago, now served as the home of a Palace—a Palace taken by Old World members and Palace-born alike.

A security officer by the name of Mark Swanson had come upon information that the cooks and teachers would be poisoning all Old World members. Like a friend would do, he alerted an older woman he'd become close with. Her name was Amy Leister.

Amy and Mark came up with a quick plan, which involved arming as many Old World members as possible in order to kill everyone working for the Order in their Palace. Mark knew where many guns could be found and had access to the keys, being a security officer. He was lucky that most of the guards were not watching the gun/ammo shed, on account of the mass poisoning being set up to happen later that night. Most of the guards were stationed at specific locations to make sure everything went off without a hitch. But, the day was going to get out of hand, and much sooner than they thought.

There were many deaths that afternoon, most of which were on the Order's side. Security officers, teachers, and the watchers in the child center had been executed. For the most part, the Palace-born followed suit once they saw what was happening. There were some who had tried defending the leadership, and they were killed for that decision. Within an hour or so, Amy, Mark, and a few others they had rallied together to complete the plan had taken the entire Palace. Now, the two ringleaders stood in the back area of the auditorium, waiting to address everyone on what the new course of action would be going forward. Neither of them knew what to say or do.

Lots of talking, some crying, and much more cheering could be heard from the auditorium. All of this seemed to make the forty-seven-year-old ex-security officer so nervous that he could not think past what they'd just accomplished. Amy could see the worry in his eyes; it was something that they both shared because they knew the enormity of what they had done, and that it would somehow get back to Sirus and the others. Amy was not willing to wallow in the fact as much as Mark.

"Would you rather me go out alone and speak to them?" Amy put a hand on the balding man's shoulder. Two poofs of gray hair sprouted up behind both of his ears, and the top of his head shined brightly. His pudgy cheeks seemed to droop downward, matching his current mood. He was not in the spirit to represent them. The people waiting on the other side of the door needed to see someone strong and driven. Mark was not the face of that, but Amy, on the other hand, was ready. The only reason she wanted to include him was because it was Mark who had brought the news of the poisoning to her and provided the weapons they used.

She could lead them, she wanted to lead them. If he was afraid, she thought it better if he sat in the crowd with everyone else. Amy thought him right for feeling the way he did about the events of the day. She didn't care though. In her opinion, everyone had received what was coming to them. If you were ready to dole out death in a cunning, unsuspecting way to good people—then you should be prepared for them to come back at you if given the opportunity.

There was no love lost with the Order and Amy. Since the first year, she knew something was very wrong with the facility and what they were being told. At first it was one year, then it was five years, then the next thing she knew, she was knocking on sixty's door and still being kept inside of the Palace..."for her own good." That's what they had said, but she didn't believe them.

Of course, she played the role, kept her profile down, but she was always waiting on an opportunity to free herself, to free her people. Just recently, she'd begun to give up on the thought of leaving the facility and someday making it back to her own house. The house she had shared with her boyfriend and their child so long ago...almost another lifetime, when she thought about it. Pieces of that life had begun to fray from her memory like pieces of a burning sheet of paper, the darkened specks flying through her mind. She was unable to form a coherent memory no matter how hard she tried.

The fear had settled inside years ago: What if she forgot everything? What if she forgot her daughter, or Joseph, her love? Time had a way of doing that, causing you to forget memories that once meant everything. Causing you to feel shame or second-guess yourself. If the memories really meant that much to her, how could she forget? How could she let the images of those she loved slip away from her?

When Mark came to her with the plan, it was like having her hope renewed. The intel he shared with her was easy for her to believe; he didn't need to convince her of the poisoning. If she was being honest with herself, a part of her didn't care if it was true or not. She wanted to rebel and get back out into the world by any means necessary. The Palace had long become a beautiful prison.

"Yeah, I think it would be best if you were to go and speak to them. I'm just not up to it." Mark exhaled deeply. "I know what we did was right. I mean, it was them or us, but still...I don't feel good about it." Mark walked to the door. He ogled out the glass at the people sitting, standing, pacing...waiting to hear what would happen next. He set his automatic rifle behind the door, made his way back to Amy, and hugged her. "This is all you, my dear."

"Don't you worry about a thing, sir. I thank you—we all thank you for your courage and that massive heart in your chest." Amy took a step back from the hug, smiling at him. She placed a hand over his chest. "Thank you. If it suits you, you can stay back here, or you can make your way around from the back here," Amy pointed at the exit behind them, "and find yourself a seat with everyone else. I'll handle the speech. Don't know what the hell I'll say, but I'll think of something." They both chuckled.

In her life before the sickness, Amy was a marketing consultant for multiple Fortune 500 companies. While new to the industry at the time, she was very successful, and she was not new to public speaking or giving people what they wanted to hear. A place like the Palace suppressed such skills, but she thought that the words and charisma could be conjured up when she found herself back in front of a room of her peers.

"I know you will, Amy. I think I'll just sit back here and watch." Mark grabbed a chair sitting at a nearby table. They were in a room that seemed as though it had been used for such times as they found themselves in today. Planning speeches, going over info and spreadsheets. There were whiteboards, dry erase markers, and a large oval-shaped table with at least twelve chairs.

Watching Mark sit in one of the chairs, Amy noticed—really noticed—his age. All of a sudden, the man seemed to be a hundred years old. She felt bad for him, and if there was more time, she would spend it soothing the thoughts going through his mind. Unfortunately, there was no time for that. There were hundreds of people outside that door, and they'd just survived a culture shock on par with what she had experienced twenty years ago. For the Palace-born people, it was their first time watching *their* world end. They would all immediately need directing.

That part was important. The need for direction was exactly how the Order was able to get her and the others to happily walk into what would be their dwelling for much longer than any of them ever thought. People just wanted to know that everything was going to be okay, whether it was or not. The precise words weren't important, just the idea behind them.

"I'll come back to check on you once this is over," Amy said to Mark without looking at him. She pulled all of her long gray hair into a ponytail at the top of her head. Her heart slowed down to a steady rate as she closed her eyes, getting into character. *Give them what they need to go on. This was only step one of the rest of our lives.* She opened the door and walked out into the auditorium to the loudest cheers she'd ever heard in her life. It reminded her of going to Yankees games with her father and uncle when she was but a child. Back in that world that no longer existed. But...the memories could be saved. That was her mission now, to save the memories of the people, and the sheer humanity from that time—before they were long forgotten.

2 2

BRANDEN

"He said that a message came over his walkie, just before I knocked him out. The message said that every Palace was being forced into Phase 2. I have no idea what that means, but I'm sure you might...Right?" He regarded Mary closely for a reaction, but her eyebrows barely even twitched. She only closed her eyes and took a deep breath.

After a few seconds, she finally spoke. "Are you sure? He said Phase 2 was being forced?" Her eyes remained shut, her face pointed up at the sky and the sun shining against her angular cheekbones. Branden couldn't help but stare at her. It was a good thing her eyes were not open and she couldn't see him studying every feature that made her what she was.

Mary's hair was the darkest color of black he'd ever seen, even darker than that. She wore what appeared to be a man's white button-down shirt and dirty green pants with pockets all over them. Branden remembered seeing the man they'd just buried wearing the same kind of pants.

"Are you sure?" she repeated.

He snapped out of his momentary hypnosis. "Yes, I'm sure. I questioned him multiple times about the same topics to see if any of the details changed. Part of a process I've formed over time with this kind of thing," Branden said with a tinge of pride in his voice. "He was telling me the truth, and that's exactly what he said to me. What is Phase 2? What exactly is a Palace? I mean, I know what they are, I've seen them before. My father told me about what the facilities looked like and that they were places where the men in the white vans took people they caught. I've never really understood why, or what goes on inside of those buildings…" Branden stopped speaking. He raised one eyebrow, wrinkling his forehead. "Can you tell me?"

Mary offered Branden a slight smile that said, *you don't want to know, young man.* Or maybe it meant…*How cute is that?* He especially did not like the latter of those thoughts he read into her smile. Branden was no child, not anymore. There was no coming back from what he'd done, what he'd enjoyed doing.

"I come from a Palace not terribly far from here. Prior to some months ago, I'd never been outside. Well, we could go outside, but not far from the building. About a hundred-yard radius around the Palace. What they told us was that everything outside of that area was contaminated with the same sickness that killed everyone twenty years ago. We believed them, and we had no reason not to. There were plenty of people who lived through that time, and they would explain how bad the sickness was. We weren't treated badly inside of the Palace; it wasn't like that—on the surface…" Mary trailed off with the last few words. Branden could see she was thinking about something.

"Hold on…if they are implementing Phase 2, that means they are trying to speed up the extermination of all Old World human life," Mary said.

"Old World? I'm so confused, Mary. What's that mean?" Branden had no idea what Mary was talking about. He'd never heard that term before. Even with context, he was in the dark.

"The Old World refers to the people who lived prior to the sickness and the ways they lived," Mary said as she got to her feet and began walking toward the gate that led to the side of the house and the front yard.

He quickly scrambled up and followed behind her, trying to keep up. "Mary, wait!" he said, grabbing her arm. She turned to face him, looking disoriented.

"If those people are called Old World, then what do they call the new people? Those born after the sickness? Please help me understand." Branden tried to catch her eyes with his own, but she was not paying attention to him.

"Um, people like me? They call us Palace-born. If you aren't Old World, then you are Palace-born. We are...kind of different from the people before the sickness." As she answered, she still wasn't focusing in on him. He could see her brain turning, thinking of something else entirely.

"So, I'm considered Palace-born? But I've never even been inside one of those things," Branden said. He felt more lost than he had when he'd set out on his own after his parents' death.

"No, silly, they would consider you Old World as well." Mary grabbed his hand, leading him to the front of the house. "Come in here. I'll share what I can, then we must go."

"Okay, because I don't know what's going on at all."

"You will, just sit down," Mary said as she opened the front door of the house. She pointed to the couch sitting against the wall, near a window with dusty white curtains.

Branden noticed the blood at the bottom of the steps when he came in, and another bloody area near the kitchen. He knew it must have been her handiwork, so it was pointless to bring it up and get even more sidetracked than they already were. He had more to tell her, but first he needed some baseline information on the situation at hand.

For the next hour, Mary sat with Branden and explained her upbringing. The Palace, the child center, the teachers, Old World members, Palace-born folk, and the different phases—at least, what she understood of them. By the end of her tale, he sat there with his eyes ajar and mouth hanging open. What she told him sounded like something from one of the books his mother would have read him when he was younger. It wasn't terribly hard to believe though; with his own eyes he had seen a huge spaceship drop from the sky—while the sky was on fire. That happened. The idea that these Palaces had been up and functioning in the world full of people for that long was worrisome.

His father never spoke much on the Palace facilities other than telling Branden to stay away from them, because even he had no information on what was going on inside. They only knew that the white vans came from the back side of them. Now he was finding out from Mary, who was human (but not really), that they were basically genetically enhancing human beings inside, and they felt no need to keep the Old World members around now that they had used them for breeding and other essential reasons.

What was more worrisome was the fact that this was widespread; the entire planet was going through this second ending of sorts. How could anyone do such a thing to people who had already suffered so much? He didn't know much about the Order, but what he did know was enough to want them gone...gone from the city, the state, the planet—hell, the entire galaxy, if what Mary told him was correct.

"There's one other thing I think you should know. I nearly forgot about it until you mentioned the guy who created the whole Palace thing," Branden said, sitting on the couch and looking at Mary. She was leaning against a small desk near the stairwell, staring at a picture of one of the family members who lived in the home before the sickness, he assumed.

Branden knew the feeling; he did the same thing every time he and his family occupied a new home. It was sad to see the faces of those who had lived in the homes, especially knowing that their remains were either still in the home or already buried or taken to the cellar of said home.

"Sirus, the so-called creator of all that we know and believe, or disbelieve, for that matter," Mary said in a mocking tone. She placed the picture face down on the desk. Branden wasn't sure, but he thought he saw her mumbling something to herself.

"What did you say?" Branden asked.

"Oh, I said Sirus, the so-called creator of all reality. I was joking, even though I do think that what he says is true. You and I both have seen evidence that says it's not completely out of the question." Mary came walking toward him again. She'd been pacing the living room during their talk for the last hour.

"No, I thought you said something after that, in a lower voice, like a mumble." His eyebrow lifted.

"Oh, nothing. Sometimes I talk to myself in my head. Talking myself through certain ideas or problems." She sat down next to him. "Tell me the thing you nearly forgot."

"Well, this Sirus guy who was somehow linked to that ship you blew out of the sky? Well, he is not dead. The gentlemen I kidnapped said that his body was removed from the battlefield, and that while he had been hurt badly, he was still alive, taken away to a different Palace."

Branden thought Mary would be pissed, but she said nothing at all. Just looked away while rubbing her hands together, as if she weren't surprised in the least. He could have sworn he saw her lips moving again. But, there were no words.

"Did he say which Palace?" Mary asked.

"No, he didn't know. I believed him."

Neither of them spoke for a few moments. They sat quietly, thinking to themselves. The day was becoming night, the clouds were becoming dark, and the sun was moving into its sleeping position. Branden had woken up that morning and started his day tracking a white van, same thing he'd done time and time again since his parents were killed. He began his work of removing them from existence, and BOOM! His life had changed forever...again.

Now he sat in an abandoned home with this woman named Mary, like the Mary from the Bible. His parents were not religious at all, but they read often, and the Bible was one of the books he'd learned. As they both sat, not speaking a word, he found himself wondering if the time he was living in was the beginning or the end. The world was in disarray, and then there was Mary, a special woman he knew would play a key role in what was to come. She'd already done as much.

Maybe he could go with her on her journey. Branden knew that he could continue to track and kill the nobodies driving the vans, or he could go with her, if she allowed it, and go after the big fish. That would give him purpose, a good purpose. Something his mother would be proud of. *I'm kind of like an apostle...She's not Jesus or anything, but she is pretty important based on the words of that soldier and what she just told me. I'm like one of her apostles. Let's hope I don't end up like her other follower who's lying in a grave in the backyard.* Branden exploded into laughter. Not at the thought of Mary's friend being dead, but of him being an apostle. He knew his father would laugh too.

The abrupt laughter startled Mary, who was off in her own world thinking, her lips slightly moving but no sound coming from them. "What's so funny?" she said, her cheeks a slight red from embarrassment.

"No, nothing...I was just thinking about something. We should try to get some rest and hit the road tomorrow before more guys come looking for you. I say we brainstorm on where Sirus's body might be? What do you think?" Branden asked, dabbing a tear from his right eye. He'd laughed harder than he thought.

"Okay, that sounds like a plan...but there is something I want to try first. We will need to find an open space and a few targets. I need to learn how to use something before I can do what I think I'm supposed to do." Mary settled back into the sofa. She smiled at Branden. "You coming along for the ride?"

"You got it." He tried to sound like it wasn't the best thing he'd heard since his parents were still alive. Inside though, his thoughts there were explosions, and bright lights shooting here and there. Branden was ecstatic that she'd invited him along on the journey she would be taking. Even though he had enjoyed his brief life being a traveling assassin of all things men-in-white-vans, it was time for a change, and time to see and do more. Those who were responsible for what happened to the world, what happened to his parents, needed to pay for their crimes. And he thought himself to be with the person that would call them to the carpet to pay for it all. "I'd love to."

23

LONNIE

EARLIER THAT MORNING, THEY'D PACKED UP A FEW BAGS OF ESSENTIALS for their short but meaningful trip. He thought he heard Simon say they were going to Lawrenceburg, Indiana, or something that sounded similar. The *where* was not important to him as much as the *how long?* He knew they didn't have much time to track Mary down, and the longer it took, the more time she would have to get farther away.

Lonnie brought a change of clothes, water canteens, and some food rations. His weapon, which was an AK-47, lay on the back seat of the white van they were riding in, its shoulder strap attached. Teacher Simon was driving, not speaking...and doing that weird finger massage thing on the steering wheel.

Lonnie was still getting accustomed to riding in a vehicle. Today made only his second time doing it, and the fast movements along with the feeling of gliding on air made him a bit queasy. Lonnie would play it off; the last thing Teacher Simon needed to know was that his young militant upstart was already sick of riding in vehicles. If he were to reach his goal of moving around the country, around the planet, getting rid of the rat rebels—he would need to handle riding in vehicles much better. In time though.

"So, I'd like to ask a few questions before we get to our destination. Is that okay?" Lonnie asked while looking to his right out the window. There were abandoned structures everywhere as far as the eyes could see. Overgrowth from trees and grass covered lots of the road signs; without the GPS, they would have no idea where they were going.

"Ask whatever your heart desires," Teacher Simon said, staring at the road in front of him. "I'll answer what I can."

Yeah, and I'm sure you will conveniently not be able to answer the "important" questions, Lonnie thought but did not say. Teacher Simon had newly renewed a healthy amount of fear within him that day in his pod, and Lonnie knew that it was not wise to tempt the man. He'd never seen him become violent in person, but he heard what Simon said that day, and there was something about his eyes. Something dark...eternal, unhappy, and swimming with knowledge.

"Thank you. I know we're going to retrieve Mary from somewhere close. I know the Order wants her, and she was obviously important to Sirus, but...why? I asked that question before, and you said that you could not answer or that it was a tough question to answer.

But I'd really like to know what makes her so important that an actual teacher would be out in the world driving around trying to find her when my squad just took back an entire Palace. What's the thing about her that has the Order so intrigued?" Lonnie turned to look at the teacher, reading the side of his sleek bony face. His bald head never seemed to have any sprouts of regrowth—it was always clean-shaven.

Lonnie could see the man's temples pulsate as if he were chewing. Teacher Simon's facial expression was blank. He did not speak right away...to Lonnie he seemed to be thinking about the answer before speaking. An intelligent habit to form.

"It's simple, Lonnie. I'm actually surprised you did not figure it out a lot sooner. I honestly did not mean that it is a tough question to answer. It would be and obviously is a tough thing for you to under-stand...or else you would already," Teacher Simon said, pausing a moment before he continued. "As I mentioned already, I am not authorized to give you this information, but seeing as we are no longer in the Palace and away from so many prying eyes—I will fill you in on what I can. Without Mary, there is no New World."

Lonnie's eyebrows lifted in surprise at that.

"It's that simple," Simon went on. "As you know, I will not be here after this all wraps up. Every teacher, watcher, and anyone else creeping in the darkest places of this planet on behalf of the Order will leave. The Palaces will be torn down after each phase has played out, and life as you know it will begin anew. You know that much, so, figuring out the importance of who and 'what' Mary is shouldn't be a shocker."

"What is she? Why is she different?" Lonnie raised his voice an octave or two. "The New World is already happening, right? I don't understand still."

Looking fixedly at Lonnie, the teacher smirked—then quickly erased the slight smile from his lips as if he'd caught himself showing too much emotion. If such a thing was even possible for him. "Are all of the Old World people eliminated?" Teacher Simon's hands still drove the car; he still stayed within the lines of the highway perfectly even though he wasn't looking at the road at all. Those empty dark eyes pierced Lonnie.

"No, not all of them just yet. But if Phase 2 has been forced all over the world, isn't it safe to say that they are being taken care of in short order?" Lonnie asked.

"Nothing is safe to say—you will learn that in your life. A job is not finalized until its finalized. You worry too much of the future and not nearly enough about the present. One can only exist if the other goes well enough." Teacher Simon turned his head, placing his eyes back on the road.

Lonnie wasn't sure if Simon even truly needed to look at the road in order for them to get to their destination. The teacher had been driving along just fine without looking for an extended amount of time, and there was little doubt that Simon would get them to their location even while staring at Lonnie with those eyes that were as dark and expansive as what lay beyond the clouds in the sky...and even farther than that. It scared Lonnie—but, he would not show it.

Showing weakness was the beginning of the end. That was a known fact.

"Okay, I can understand that. I'm even interested in doing all I can in order to help find and kill all the rats. I want that to be my job going forward...after this, I mean." He looked out the window once again. They drove past an exit that had a shopping mall and a humongous plaza. Lonnie knew what they were called because he'd seen them in videos. He could remember learning about those in morning enrichment classes. It was hard to imagine that place—or any place—filled with actual people. There were so few in the world he'd found after coming out of the Palace.

Once Melinda had brought up going to buy clothes in one of them when the world returned to its prior self. The thought of Melinda made Lonnie feel badly, and so he tried to not think of her as much as possible. She was a dumb girl who had listened to her heart more than her own mind, and for that she had lost her life. He was not to be trusted, no one was—that was her mistake, trusting him. Lonnie took the thought and mushed it down into the core of his being, the same place where all of the dark memories or thoughts he'd rather not think about lived. The memory of the young woman Michelle rotting in the pod lived in that same place. That had been the beginning of it all for him.

"Your aspirations are known, and I'm here to help you meet them." Teacher Simon took an exit, the sign for which Lonnie could not read. "Try to stay focused on what we are here for. The last information we received on Mary's whereabouts, she was engaged by some of our people. As I told you, all communication stopped with them, so it's assumed they were killed," Teacher Simon said.

"But, how do we know that? They could have captured or murdered her." Just the thought of that made his stomach do a cartwheel. Thinking that someone else would get the praise and adulation of catching Mary...oh, special Mary.

Everything inside of him wished that was not the case. The palms of his hands began to itch, a nervous tick he'd developed from his time growing up in the child center. Lonnie rubbed them on his pants to soothe the itching without actually scratching them. He knew Teacher Simon would notice how nervous he was becoming. Probably already had.

Teacher Simon gazed at him once more. "I have my ways of knowing. She has not been captured or killed. If this was the case, Lonnie, we would not be on our way to finish the job ourselves." He turned onto a street littered with broken-down cars. Weeds grew through the cement, ensnaring the wheels of each vehicle. Slowly, they drove down the street. Lonnie frantically surveyed his surroundings, wondering if Mary was in the area. He thought not because he hadn't been told to get his gun ready. With that thought, he reached back into the back seat to grab the AK-47.

"Don't bother," Teacher Simon said.

"Why not? If she is he—"

"She is not here. We are here for different reasons altogether. This will go more smoothly if you keep your mouth shut and take direction. You are not the commander of this mission, young man. You are no more than a puppy in a game riddled with ferocious full-grown wolves. You cannot and will not ever understand the scope of what's going on around you. Even in the spaces you cannot see. Be happy to be along for the ride; you will get your credit when all is said and done." Teacher Simon pulled into the driveway of a house. It was the only house Lonnie had ever seen with a mowed lawn.

The hedges were trimmed, and there was a welcome mat in front of the door. "Listen and learn if you ever want to be the leader you already believe yourself to be. Leave the weapons inside the vehicle and follow me." Teacher Simon opened the driver side door of the van and stepped out. Lonnie followed. Before they could close their doors, someone opened the door of the house. It was an older woman, and she was smiling.

24

MARY

FRUSTRATION WAS NOT THE WORD. RAGE WAS PROBABLY MORE OF AN accurate description of what she felt at that moment. She'd used the stupid weapon twice now, and when she had, it felt as normal as breathing. The way she synced with the object had been effortless in those moments, the moments when she really didn't think about it. Then, there were times when she wanted to use the weapon...the thing Sirus had called a Lohar weapon. But nothing happened...she couldn't get it to react to her. No smoke, no flicker of a flame, no heat...nothing. The rock seemed to look up at her from the palm of her hand with a face that said, "Trick no good, try again."

Mary and Branden found a junkyard-looking area of old broken appliances and cars, mostly cars. Branden said it would be good for her to practice with the weapon in a place like that. Lots to destroy, and it was out of the way, so she would not draw any unwanted attention from Palace-born soldiers still on the hunt for her.

Explaining to him what the weapon was (from what she understood) did not take as much time as she thought it would. Branden was quick; he understood and accepted new concepts with little explanation. It helped that he had seen the ship fall from the sky with his own eyes. Something had to have made that much destruction, and he knew enough about weapons to know that no gun could do such a thing.

Branden sat on the hood of a rusted-out 2012 Chevy Impala. His feet rested on the front bumper of the car with his hands behind him, balancing his body on the hood. She could see from her peripheral vision that he was trying not to look at her, so his face pointed to the darkening orange hue of the sky. Evening was approaching, and it was best to do any practicing before dark fell over the day.

Mary thought Branden was considerate for looking away during her failed attempts of using the weapon. It would be more stressful if he was gawking at her from his perch on the car twenty or so yards away.

She switched the object to her other hand, closing the fingers of her left hand around it tightly. It was about the size of a child's fist; not terribly large. She thought back to walking toward the Eagle squad meeting on the field the day before, the weapon banging against her knee with every step. Mary didn't know what it was at the time— and her late friend Dale would not allow her to look—but that morning, she had used the power encapsulated inside of the Lohar weapon easily enough.

Mary closed her eyes and strained her mind to focus in on the thing in her left hand. She had no idea what she was doing exactly, and she felt dumb. There would be no real progress made in her mission to remove the threat of the Order from the world without the use of the only weapon that could truly hurt them. Obviously, that would be assuming that the teachers had the same weaknesses Sirus had, but there was no reason to believe any different. The security guards were human, the Palace-born were mostly human, so—normal bullets would dispatch them. She knew that there needed to be maximum damage created in order to remove the true threats, and only the weapon in her hand could do that. She forced herself to be calm and focused…

You will never figure it out, Mary. Because you don't want to…accept what you are, Sirus said. Instead of focusing in on his random banter, Mary thought about Jacob. For a long time she tried not to go there.

Even more than the children she left behind in the Palace and the one taken from her months ago by the insane zealot in the rebel Palace, Jacob's memory was the top source of pain in her soul. *What soul? Hahaha...*

The beginning of her journey to find freedom, to discover the truth of herself and the planet, had begun with Jacob. He'd been the first to get her to think for herself, to push her when she did not want to be pushed. The life they had planned to have after escaping the Palace was cut short by one single gunshot.

She could still see the moment in her head with such clarity that her dreams would never be normal again. Mary could remember slowly turning around while running, almost running backwards in order to see why Jacob was no longer close enough for her to hear his loud breathing while running. That small moment was the fastest and most exhilarating happiness she'd ever experienced. So close, and so far away at the same time.

Just as she had turned to look, there he was, lying in the grass face down, his back rising and falling quickly. With each breath came another spurt of blood from a small hole right between his shoulder blades. She still remembered how beautiful the grass of the Palace was that day. Mary always thought remembering the details of the grass during that moment was odd. Why did she even notice how amazing and well-kept the grass was while running to Jacob to help him?

It's funny, the whimsical details we notice in the most traumatic moments of life. Or...maybe he wasn't as important to you as you'd like to think. There is that.

"Shut up, Sirus," Mary said aloud, but not loud enough for Branden to hear her.

After flipping Jacob's body over to see his face, to kiss him, to compel him to get up and make a final push for the forest not far from where they were, she'd noticed his face...those eyes. Blood and gore poured from his lips as he tried to get the words out—the last words he would ever say to her. He'd told her to go, to run away and save herself. Then his eyes moved to the clouds along with his soul. Just like that, everything in the world stopped and became quiet. Jacob lay there, looking as peaceful as someone having a picnic, staring up at the sky after filling up on sandwiches and drinks.

Going back to that place with Jacob caused her to become sullen, beyond enraged, and saddened. In that very moment, if she could burn the world to ashes, she would have. Thinking about it there in the dump with Branden had the same effect on her. She could feel her body heating up, and the hand with which she grasped the weapon trembled. The tendons in her neck were standing at attention; she could feel them tightening so hard that her temple began to throb with the beginnings of a headache.

Standing there surrounded by hundreds of cars, the smell of old oil and rust permeated throughout. Mary could hear small animals in their nests, moving around underground in the homes they had dug. Feeding their young, scurrying here and there. She could even hear Branden's silent reaction—could hear his heartbeat and the fact that he was holding his breath as he waited on her to do the trick she'd explained to him only an hour or two before.

Her focus was pinpoint, the entire area became clearer in that moment. There was a fire in her belly stirring, and just when she could feel her right hand beginning to get warm…nothing happened.

Mary felt defeated. All that build-up for nothing at all. She screamed as loud as she could and flung the object though the windshield of an SUV to her right. Everything she could hear and feel in the environment just moments before became blotted out by the shattering of the windshield. No longer could she hear Branden's breathing or the small rodents and other animals hidden away in the dark crevices of the dump. The flutter of a butterfly's wings went silent as the unclear loudness of the world came rushing back, bursting into her ears.

Mary collapsed to her knees, her legs splayed out beneath her like a baby deer learning to walk only minutes after leaving its mother's womb. Her long unmanageable hair covered her face and shoulders as she cried into the dirt beneath her. *It's just too hard, I can't do it…*Her own thoughts of the impossibility of figuring out the Lohar weapon came to the surface. Maybe she never would.

25

BRANDEN

HE WALKED OVER TO HER BECAUSE HE KNEW SHE WAS STRUGGLING. HE'D been there many times in his own life. Not to the extent that she was now, but he could remember not being able to figure out the bow and arrows his father created. For a long time, he had no idea how to hold the damn thing correctly. When he used the bow, the makeshift arrow flew everywhere but in the direction he aimed. To the right, the left, sometimes even in the sky. There were times he thought he would never be able to hunt with his parents. Times where he thought he would never be helpful to them.

"Mary...get up," Branden said from behind her. She did not answer; her head was aimed toward the ground with her legs bent beneath her awkwardly and her hands in the dirt. The white shirt she wore blew behind her with the wind, now showing light brown stains from the dirt on the ground.

"Let me try to help you out with this. Sometimes a different point of view or set of eyes can help unlock something you didn't think of." Branden bent his knees slowly, placing both hands in the dirt while sitting on his butt next to Mary.

Without looking up or at him, Mary flicked a rock with her thumb and spoke in a childish tone. A defeated and frustrated tone. "It's not going to work. I've been struggling with that damned thing since I've had it." She sounded repulsed by the small weapon that now sat in the front of the black SUV not far from them. "I'm beginning to think it only works when it wants to. I've tried everything."

For a moment Branden didn't respond; he didn't want her to think he was challenging her knowledge on something she knew much more about—something he just found out existed today. After a little time, he spoke up softly. "I can understand that, and you may even be right about that. Something so powerful could very well have a mind of its own. I could see that." Branden had learned how to be agreeable while also saying his piece from his Mother. She was the smartest and kindest person, and she'd used the tactic on him and his father alike. Worked every time. Agree and sprinkle in a bit of advice on your way out. That was how she did it.

"Can I ask you a question though, Mary?"

Branden could hear her blowing beneath her breath while her shoulders slumped even more. He could see that she was becoming annoyed. "Yes, Branden, what would you like to ask me?"

"I was just wondering…have you thought about the conditions of your psyche the two times that you have successfully used the weapon? Like, what was going on in your mind and around you?" Branden spoke casually while picking up a handful of small stones and tossing them at a dented Maytag washer.

"I was angry. I told you that earlier. The two times I've used it, I was highly wrathful. Now, for some reason me being angry doesn't work anymore." Mary's eyes were desperate when she took in the sight of him. Her cheeks were bright red. She wiped tears from her eyes as she flipped her hair away from her face.

"Oh yeah…I remember you saying that. You are right, you did tell me." Branden flicked another rock toward the washer, trying to make it inside of the open lid. "Was there anything else though? Were you feeling sad and fiery? Or maybe, say, scared and angry? Maybe there is another emotion going on inside of you that activates the thing?" Branden said.

Mary looked around the dump, obviously trying to calm herself—

she was clearly vexed at being questioned about something she was clearly trying very hard at figuring out. He knew what she was thinking: *What do you think you can mention that I haven't already thought of?* It's what he would have been thinking himself.

"Nothing, I was just furious and I...I just really wanted to kill the men I was infuriated with at the time. Sirus the first time, and the three men responsible for killing Dale the second. I was really angry, and I wanted them...dead. Badly. I was just really incensed, if that makes sense? That's all I remember thinking." Mary used her hands to hoist herself up from the ground, then dusted her dirty palms off on the thighs of her pants. Branden rose to his feet along with her.

"I wonder though," Branden said while motioning her to walk with him toward the SUV, where the object likely lay on the floor of the vehicle.

"What?" Mary said, walking alongside of him.

"What if, in order to use the weapon, you need to feel hateful enough that you want to kill? Like, really hurt someone?" Branden stopped speaking for a moment, allowing Mary to take in his words. "Seems like in both instances, you had people in front of you who had taken the lives of people you cared for, or at least respected." Branden opened the door of the SUV after a few hard yanks of the handle.

Mary said nothing. He could see her thinking through the cracked glass of the windshield. She stood in front of the vehicle, and again her lips were moving, but nothing was coming out of her mouth. Branden recalled her saying that she figured out problems that way, by mouthing situations or solutions to herself. Everyone had their weird quirks, he supposed. "What do you think?" He poked his head above the passenger door and stared at her.

"It's possible, but I don't know. I had the weapon in my pocket when I killed the two Palace soldiers inside of the house before Dale was killed. I didn't feel it react to me at that time...and I wanted them to die," she said, seeming to snap out of a deep-thinking trance.

"Yeah, that's true. But you didn't say they came after you though. So really, how truly chafed were you at the time?" Inside, Branden's heart warmed at the word *chafed*. It was a word his mother had said often. He didn't know what made him choose that word, but he knew it would bring a smile to his mother's face if she were there to hear it.

"From what you told me," he went on, "they were pretty easy kills, as they had no previous ideas about what you were capable of. Also, they hadn't killed anyone that you cared for...I'm not sure if that last thing is a part of what makes the weapon work for you. It's just a thought."

"Yes...that's true. I don't think that I had the same disdain and murderous intentions for the two inside the house. The female soldier even pulled a move on me, and I took her easily," Mary said. Then her lips made more silent movements just before she rolled her eyes.

Why does she do that? What's going on inside of her? Branden wondered to himself, but he didn't say anything. He thought Mary was on the verge of figuring something out for herself.

"But, if that's true..." Mary paused. "That means that I need to be in an offensive murderous frenzy in order to use the thing." She said it more to herself than to him.

"Could that be possible?" Branden asked.

"I...don't...I don't know. I hope not." Mary appeared to be embarrassed and she looked away from him. Neither of them said anything for a minute.

"Look, it's getting late. We don't have to figure it out right now. Let's find the weapon and get into one of these houses. We should sleep and talk more on the subject when we wake up. What do you think?" Branden poked his head into the SUV and began searching for the odd-shaped object. Mary said nothing at all.

TEACHER SIMON

SIMON STROLLED PAST THE OLD WOMAN AS IF HER HOME WAS HIS OWN. In more ways than a few, that was exactly the case. She didn't seem offended by his walking past her and directly into the house. Lonnie reluctantly followed him, smiling at the woman and thanking her.

Simon stood in the middle of the living room, watching Lonnie, wondering how the kid would reconcile all that he'd learned about people from the Old World. He'd been trained to kill them, and now he was having to control his combat urges. Simon hadn't told him not to hurt the woman, just that they were there to see someone—and he was acting accordingly based on cues from whom he now understood to be the leader, Simon. That was good; confusion was the root of mistakes, and mistakes cost lives more than not.

The home was illuminated by golden shimmers of light from the candles that were everywhere. There was no electricity, so that made sense. Laila was waiting on him, like he'd told her to do so long ago. There was a large brown sofa pushed against the far west wall of the room and a fireplace with darkened, chipped pieces of wood, long burned out. The flooring of the room was hardwood, but there was a large oval-shaped rug in the middle of the floor decorated with Native-looking nonsense. One look at the room's decor and the beaded dreadlocks in Laila's hair told Simon all he needed to know about the person she'd become since their last talk.

Some in the Old World would call her a witch doctor, or a shaman —someone who dealt in holistic medicines and cures. The scent of exotic spices, flowers hanging from thin pieces of rope from the ceiling, and scented candles fogged the air of the house. He'd smelled them the moment they pulled up.

"Have a seat, gentleman." Laila spoke in a soft, inviting voice. Her face was as pleasant as the first time he'd seen her, but now it was filled with age lines and creases. The eyes were still special though. Those were the single detail that had first attracted him to use her— the deep-set, sparkling hazel eyes. They remained as enchanting as they'd been the day he looked upon her inside of the beautiful hand-made crib on her first birthday.

Even then, those eyes made him jealous. Where he came from, the eyes meant everything, for they were actual windows. Not to the soul, but to all things that could be fathomed, and even the unfathomable.

"Thank you, Laila, I think I'll stand." He noticed her eyebrows twitch upward when he'd said her name. Inside, she knew it was him, but the human consciousness was always on the cliff of doubt until assurance came to nudge them off. The act of Simon simply saying her name brought her into a freefall of one hundred percent surety. "But, our young friend Lonnie here would be happy to sit."

Simon motioned for the young man to take a seat on the brown sofa with a halfhearted lift of his hand in that direction. Lonnie complied. The boy's face was confused, and there was a hint of fear. But why? Why was he afraid? For some time now, he'd not been around someone from the Old World without trying to knock off parts of their body with an automatic weapon. A shock of some sort maybe? The psychology of it was interesting to him, but they had come there for a particular reason. He'd question Lonnie about it on their way to retrieve Mary.

"I knew you'd come," Laila said to Teacher Simon, walking toward him. He stared down at the woman who stood at least two and a half feet shorter than him. "You said that you would, and here are you are."

Her beautiful hazel eyes began to sparkle and crack into a trillion pieces of glass as tears fell.

Simon reached down to her hand, which at that point was on its way in the direction of his face. He knew she wanted to touch him, but he had no intentions of bending down to meet that heartwarming show of affection. His monstrous hand swallowed hers as he turned his back and led her to a white rocking chair. Over the years, it had aged so much that the paint was splintered and cracking all over. He knew it was the only chair in the home she'd spent any time sitting in...thinking about him, even more than she thought about the two daughters she'd lost during the sickness.

The father of both girls had left them years before the end. He was what some would call a rolling stone, never seeing Laila as an actual option to live life with, but more so for coupling companionship. Such was the routine for men and women during that time. Served her right for testing his words anyway. She knew that the sickness was coming, because he'd told her as much many times during her lifetime. The last time being when she was twelve, when he had given her a special job.

Laila sat down in slow motion. First her legs bent (and cracked), then her back did as much bending as one would expect a seventy-year-old woman's back to bend (while also cracking) before she sat down hard in the chair—compelling the poor old thing to do some of its own screeching as her old bones rocked it backwards. She let out a tired gasp as her body settled into the seat. The whole ordeal played out like a theatric interpretation of settling down in old age. Simon looked down upon her without smiling...but there was a bit of pity in his expression.

Lonnie sat there on the sofa with his hands placed on both knees. The headstrong militant would-be god of the New World was again a child. He looked every bit of his young adult self, nothing for anyone to fear. Being around ones elders had that effect on most everyone. The boy stayed quiet as he surveyed the room and all of the knick-knacks, flowers, and family items he'd never seen before. Simon wasn't sure if he was paying attention...soon he would though.

"You...haven't aged...a day." She spoke in small gasps; the sitting had taken much out of her. She was still too young to be so sickly and tired, he thought, but considering what she'd been though in her life, he would guess her true age to be closer to one hundred years old if all the wear and tear on her body and mental pain was to be quantified. "Wish I could say the same for myself. What's your secret, Simon?" Laila smiled widely, exposing her still-straight white teeth.

"Magic, of course." Simon winked at her while positioning himself to stand in front of her. With her foot, Laila softly pushed off the floor, creating momentum to get the chair rocking back and forth. With both hands on the arms of the chair, she gazed into his eyes. He thought that she would do that until she starved to death if he didn't snap her out of the fixation she had going.

"I owe you my appreciation for following directions." Simon forced a thin-lipped smile.

"Oh no, thank you," she replied. "And you don't have to smile. I know it's not your way. Everything that you ever told me came to be, just the way that you said it would. I should have heeded your advice long ago to not create life—but even with my unflinching faith in your words, a young woman of eighteen could not be talked out of love."

Laila's head leaned back as one of her hands shot up to point at the pictures displayed on the wall shelf behind her chair. The pictures were those of her two daughters. Many pictures all clustered together —it reminded Simon of a shrine. Many had been created in his name, his many names. Civilizations for millions of years in infinite worlds praised him in the same ways that she did for her children.

"They are beautiful...all was not terrible, I'm sure. You deserved to experience that in your lifetime."

"Kind words, I thank you. I would've just as well not experienced the pain that came along with losing them. I was warned of what would come, and I didn't care...and for that I paid. No fault of yours, Simon." Resting her head on the small pillow strapped to the top of the chair's back, she exhaled deeply and smiled again.

"You were always wise beyond your years. The stones that I asked you to bury in the ground were found and used for what they were intended. That is because of you. Even back then, I knew you could be trusted to take care of it for me. My thanks belong to you, Laila.

"Even at that age, you did what most would not have done. I know it must have been hard to live most of your life with the burden of knowing the world would be ending and you would live through it while losing everyone around you. Your back had to be strong to endure such a burden." Simon's long arm swung forward, allowing his fingers to touch hers. He grabbed on to one of her hands and squeezed it, never allowing his eyes to lose track of hers.

"I'd be lying if I said it wasn't hard…and you'd know I was lying, so I won't. It was hard, but it gave me purpose. You gave me purpose," Laila said.

"How many stones were buried there?" Simon asked.

"Just the two in the bag that I awoke to in my bed one morning. I buried the entire bag. Only once did I look inside—there were two. I didn't look again before burying them, for obvious reasons. The contents felt powerful, magical. It made me feel physically weak." Laila's hand moved within his own. He could feel her small fingers trying to caress his palm.

Simon turned his head to check on Lonnie. The boy only watched, his mouth agape at the news of finding out that the old woman sitting in the rocking chair before him was the person responsible for the weapon that had been used to destroy Sirus's manifestation link. He would not speak, he could not—the child only watched. *Good, watch and learn. Realize what you are in the scheme of things, which is nothing.*

Directing his focus back on Laila, he spoke again. "No one ever found out about this, did they? The stones, or our relationship?" Simon said.

"No, never. My entire life, you were the man in my dreams who told nothing but the truth…the one who gave knowledge." Laila sounded panicked, as if she would cry if he did not believe her words.

"Good, good. Did you ever have dreams of someone else? Someone like me? Or even voices in your head?" Simon probed her for information, wondering if Sirus had figured out his deception.

There would come a time when he would have to face the other half of their union. If Sirus had an idea who placed the Lohar weapons into the created reality, he would make many problems for Simon going forward. The headache was not needed; Simon only needed the Earth exercise to come to an end sooner rather than later. Or at the very least, to become self-sustainable without his presence being needed to counter Sirus's insatiable desire for attention and praise.

"Never...only you."

She said the words with confidence. There was no hitch in her voice, no movement in the pupils. Lies were simple things to decipher even without using his own abilities. The specimens he and Sirus created together had a fail-safe implemented into their DNA that would give off some type of unnoticeable telltale sign when they were not being truthful to the best of their knowledge. Subliminally or otherwise.

"I'm happy to hear that. Thank you, Laila." Simon released her hand after guiding it back to the arm of the chair. He could see in her eyes that she was saddened by that. If allowed, she would hold on to him until they both turned to dust; they both knew that.

"What would make you happy? Your purpose has come to an end, and I find you here living alone, dying slowly in a dwelling too big for your small body. Surrounded by memories of ghosts from the world before. Our time together has come to an end, so before I walk out that door...what can I do for you?" His voice was sincere. He meant what he said...the choice was given, but there was only one outcome for her. Only one thing made sense—one gift was best for her.

For a moment, she looked away from him, looking around the house at the things she'd enclosed around her life. Taking them all in, smiling the entire time, Laila's eyes finally found Simon's once more. "I just want to go home now. My life's promise has been completed, and now I'm so tired, Simon. I want to go home now that I've pleased you." Tears came back to the surface of her eyes. They rolled slowly down her cheeks.

Simon nodded before reaching out with a finger to stop her tears. He bent down on one knee to get eye level with Laila, then took both her hands within his own there on her lap. The rocking chair came to a stop. He could have accomplished what he planned to do without bending down, but he wanted Lonnie to witness it.

SIMON PEERED INTO HER EYES, really looked into them…inside of them. Each flicker of his pupil became larger in Laila's mind until she felt as though she were floating in space all alone with no protective suit. Images of every real or possible outcome her life could have taken flashed in her psyche all at once…

She saw the instance of her older brother creeping into her room to touch her in the places Mother said were not good.

She saw every time a man took advantage of her in college, when she was made to suffer through their heavy breathing and pushing inside of her. The times when friends would come over to join in the fun when she'd drunk too much. All of the faces were as crisp in her mind as they would have been if they were in the room with her right then…if she were still in a room. There was nothing but darkness and flickers of pain.

Then she witnessed every car accident that left her decapitated, every time her mother or father murdered her. Each time the same touchy brother came into her room to open her throat with his pocket knife. The millions of times she was jumped from behind by a man and was beaten to death. Those things never occurred in the version of her life that she could remember, but at the same time—they did.

A version of her had experienced all of it. In that moment, Laila realized that she was seeing the memories of every version of herself in every reality possible. A million parallel universes with a million Laila's, all experiencing EVERY possible outcome.

The flashes of successful Laila, of thriving Laila—they were there of course, but those images were dull in comparison to the traumatic events flashing by her eyelids while being trapped inside of the black hole that made up the endless depths of Simon's eyes.

Laila thought that she wanted to live inside of him, to be a part of the space she saw inside through the windows on his face. Her entire life she had dreamed of it, obsessed about being with him. And not in a romantic way, but to just be *of* him. The things that she could learn from Simon—even scratching the surface of his knowledge would be enough for her brain to dine on for hundreds of years.

Since the age of thirty-four, after her last shot at finding love in the world, Laila had committed herself to becoming one with the planet. Doing all things in a holistic fashion, preparing both her mind and body for the time when he would return to her. To take her away. She wasn't sure exactly where, but if it was with or within him...that would be home. How dense she'd turned out to be in the end.

She could now see that what made up the "thing" within him was...it was infinite. And without perspective or aim. There was no good or bad—there were simply outcomes, and every outcome that could ever be...continuously. Forever. It was something that had no beginning or end, because swimming around in his eyes made her feel constant terror that would never stop.

Laila now knew what lay beyond the veil of her greatest wishes, and now she only wanted to close her eyes forever—but she could not. She wanted to be back inside of her home, in her rocking chair again...but how long had it been since she was there? The answer was lost on her. Had it been minutes? Years? Centuries or lifetimes? The answer was none and all of them at the same time. Watching yourself die a billion times for a billion years without blinking was something that no one should have to live through, yet she was doing just that.

No matter how hard she tried, her eyes would not close. The feeling of being forced to watch the most torturous things you could imagine drove her crazy. Somewhere out in the world, in a physical plane where she could still feel something, she reached out to that person—the woman who was sitting in her home, in her rocking chair, speaking to Simon.

Reaching out to the physical form of herself, if that person still existed, she did the only thing she could think of. Laila became wildly insane inside of Simon's eyes, and it was a wonder that the thought made sense to her to do what came next.

LONNIE

LONNIE WATCHED AS THE TWO ONLY STARED AT EACH OTHER. IT couldn't have been any longer than two minutes, if that. No one spoke, especially not him. He'd said nothing since walking into the house. Teacher Simon was down on one knee, holding on to her hands as the woman he called Laila stared at him. There was a goofy grin on her face, and she looked utterly blissful.

At first.

Then, like night and day, everything changed. Laila's lips slowly curled into a disgusting frown. The flaps that were once cheeks hung low, covering the laugh lines on her face. Her eyebrows arched down-ward...but the joy in her eyes never left. The sight was unbelievable; he'd never seen a face wear two different expressions at once, but there it was. Right in front of him. Teacher Simon had bent down in order for him to see—he knew that now.

Laila's mouth opened wider than a human's mouth should; nothing would make him believe that her bottom jaw did not become unhinged. Lonnie had seen fish open their mouths that wide, but no human would be able to pull it off. Not even close.

He dug his nails into the material of the brown couch, unaware that his body was shrinking into the closest thing that resembled a ball while sitting. His legs were as close together as possible, and his shoulders crept closer together, pushing his chest muscles in. The sight of Laila caused him to want to fold into himself.

There was a crackling sound coming from her mouth, deep within her throat. The sound reminded him of a crackling fire. Small snapping and popping sounds emitted from her throat before she eventually screamed—loud enough to burst his eardrums. Lonnie's hands quickly left the cushions of the brown sofa and flew to the sides of his head as fast as they could to cover his ears. The sound reminded him of the day the ship fell from the sky. Teacher Simon never flinched; he simply continued to gaze deeply into her eyes and hold on to her small, fragile hands.

Her own eyes still looked elated to be in his presence, but now there was blood beginning to emerge from them. Laila's nose began to bleed, and the sides of her mouth tore open. Lonnie covered his eyes with one of his hands, removing it from his ear. But the sound of the scream—the constant scream—caused him to think better of that decision. Lonnie couldn't look at what was happening to Laila, and he couldn't remove his hands from his ears…so he watched.

There was a part of him that did not want to see. And an insanely curious part of him that did, and that part won the decision. Laila pulled her hands free from Simon's loose grip and immediately began scratching and gouging at her eyes. The whole while she screamed. Rocking in the chair, she screamed and dug into the pits of her eyes. Simon stood up, breaking his gaze with her as he looked toward the window there in the living room. There was nothing out there but the sunrays of the early afternoon. At least that's what Lonnie assumed— though he could see nothing but her.

By the time the screaming ceased, Laila's face was a raggedy, open wound of its former self. There were no eyes to speak of; those lay on the floor next to her chair. In their place were purplish, mushy holes. Some of her fingers were broken, snapped at the joints from the violent digging and scratching. Her arms dangled on the sides of the chair she still sat in. She was gone…but the chair slowly rocked back and forth.

By the time Lonnie realized that Teacher Simon had left the home and was sitting in the car waiting for him to collect his thoughts and join him, the day had crept into evening. Lonnie realized that he'd sat in the living room of Laila's home with her dead body for hours without knowing it. Feeling as though he'd just woken up, he stood, balanced himself on the arm of the sofa, then walked out the front door.

PART III

COME BACK

28

MARY

Not far from the dump, she and Branden found a cul-de-sac of beautiful homes just outside of a wooded area. They chose the closet house and walked right through the front door, which was unlocked. By that time, the sun had all but retreated, and the moon was materializing in the sky. Darkness was bad for them, and it was good for those who were hunting her.

Branden said they would have goggles or glasses that allowed them to see in the dark. The man he'd extracted information from had glasses like that. When asked by Mary why he didn't take the soldier's equipment, Branden answered, "Because I have my own shit to carry." They both laughed, ate some jerky he did have with his own shit, and lay down on the bottom floor of the house.

He'd fallen asleep almost instantly. It had been a long day for the young man, and she was sure that the things he'd learned weighed on his mind, even if he pretended nothing shook or surprised him. As for Mary, sleep would be the elusive bastard it had always been for her. Only now there was no Jacob to ease her mind and body before it was time to turn in.

Mary's thoughts took over. Well...her thoughts, and those of a certain someone else who had been doing his best to annoy her since she'd run away from the battlefield. He would not allow any down-time in her mind, and she wondered if Branden thought her to be insane yet. The young man had no doubt seen her talking to herself more than once. With all that he'd learned in the past twenty-four hours, she thought the alien girl with special powers mumbling quips to herself was the least of his worries. The thought brought a smile to her face.

Branden lay snoring on the floor next to the oversized loveseat she had settled into. He'd covered himself with a comforter from one of the beds upstairs. He'd brought down two, one for each of them, and directed her not to go up there. The family who owned the home was still up there...not alive, of course, but their bodies remained.

Apparently, his family had moved around, staying in homes much like the one they were in tonight. Finding bodies of the previous owners was not a rare thing; he was accustomed to seeing them and getting rid of their remains in a respectful way. He told Mary that as soon as morning came, he would do just that with the family in this home. He was good to have around, if for no other reason than to have someone to talk to. Advice from him wasn't bad either—the thing he'd said about the Lohar weapon was possible.

The idea of NEEDING to be a savage animal in order to use it made her wonder if she could continue to wield such a thing. The fear of changing her base self in order to call upon the Lohar weapon's power was a real concern.

No...not call upon its power, Mary, but to help you harness your own.

And there he was, placing doubt and confusion within her every thought.

Maybe if you would stop trying to pretend that you aren't hearing me, I could be of some use to you. You coming to hate me is irrelevant to what's going on in your life right now and your future plans. Being hated by your children is common...I would know, I have many. Sirus spoke clearly in her mind, so clear that it was a wonder the volume did not wake Branden—but it was all in her head.

Mary had pondered earlier in the day if she was going crazy. Had the years of mental trauma coupled with watching Jacob die, then losing their child, all bundled up with murdering sixty-plus people on the Palace field driven her mad? She didn't *feel* insane though; she felt like herself. Except now she heard the voice of a man she'd killed, and he didn't even sound angry about it. Even though when she used the weapon on his ship he'd screamed like his guts were being pulled through one of his nostrils.

Mary decided to have a short back-and-forth with the voice in her head. Whether it was actually Sirus or a part of her own psyche, it might help. And things couldn't get worse.

Lying there on the loveseat, she finally closed her eyes and spoke back in her mind...trying to understand, not fight. How did one fight a voice from within anyway?

Explain what you mean without all the riddles and vague nonsense, Mary said to the voice within.

Of course, Sirus answered. *I can't tell you anything that you don't already know. It's less about explaining myself and more about you accepting what you are.*

But, what am I? Am I human, am I something else entirely? What did you do to me? she asked.

What you are is not important. What is anything but cells and other scientific terms and theories that don't mean anything in the scheme of things? Would you feel better if you were weaker? Capable of less? Destined to be nothing more than another mundane walking bag of blood and bone with a lifespan that is no more than a flicker in comparison to the history of all things? Do you want to be nothing? Sirus's voice became harsher as he trudged deeper into his soliloquy. Listening to him speak from his proverbial soapbox brought back memories of the time he'd lectured her and Jacob, before he pretended to let them leave together.

Mary didn't know how to answer his questions without sounding entitled or showing signs of self-importance—things she'd been counseled against her entire life. And now here she was, talking to the program director—who was apparently one half of her DNA makeup —and he was making a case for her to be the exact opposite. *Why...are you saying this? Why would you want me to learn to use a weapon like that? I saw what it did to you,* Mary said.

Eh, I'm fine. And someday I'll be back. But let's just say, I have my reasons. Those reasons are of no importance to you at this point; focus more on the fact that our goals are aligned. You want to be this gallant hero that drives the evil of the Order back into oblivion or wherever it is that you think we come from, and I wouldn't mind seeing you do that.

To Mary, it sounded like he was smiling. She didn't respond, and he continued. *I made you different for a reason. Ninety-nine percent of what I said to you and Jacob was true. Your planet is in the process of rebooting, and there needs to be someone to lead the New World into the future. That person is and always has been you. Why do you think I wanted to get you back so desperately?* Sirus laughed, and the echo vibrated in her head, causing her temples to pulse a bit.

I have a tendency to involve myself in things more than I should, he said. *That's okay though, it's not the first time and probably won't be the last. Point is, no matter what you do, you will never escape your purpose. Accept who and what you are in order to do what you need to do.*

Mary spoke up then. *Why are you a proponent of me destroying the Order all of a sudden? First you wanted to push me into going back into the fray, which would have led to my capture or death—and...now you are my biggest cheerleader to take the Order out.* She felt bewildered. There was an angle that benefited him more than her, that was obvious. She thought of something else. *Am I a killer? Is that why I'm so good at it? Are you saying to take pride or happiness in taking lives? Is that truly what makes the Lohar weapon react to me?*

I'm a proponent of my creation, he said. *Not only you, but everything continuing...My slight change in direction is not for you to worry about. You worry too much. Stick to your own mission, which is what I'm helping you with as we speak. Accept it in blind faith.*

And Mary, he went on, *as for you being a killer and enjoying the work of killing...Don't you? Tell me truthfully that you do not enjoy it. You can't. What you must understand, Mary, is that we all are exactly what we are. It's not about good and bad; these constructs don't exist anywhere but in your own mind. Do what comes naturally to you, as that's the design. That is, if you want what you say you do. Because if you don't stop them, it will all be over.* There was a tinge of desperation in his voice.

Mary could see that he was in some kind of bind where he NEEDED her to get rid of the Order for him. It was clear that she had not killed him, but for some reason he only lived in her mind. There was something in his tone that told her there was much more to his sudden change of heart.

For the next hour, she spoke to Sirus in her mind. Without audibly saying a word, they had a palaver and she learned. She accepted, not because he convinced her, but because there was no convincing needed. Mary had felt what she was long before the battle outside the rebel Palace. Carla had lit the flame in her belly upon their first meeting, and that was the day Mary knew. Somewhere deep inside, she knew.

That night, speaking to Sirus, listening to him twist lies and the truth, she decided to accept that in order to bring the world some peace again...she needed to be herself. At the end of the heart-to-heart, he told her that he would not be able to speak to her for a while. There were things that needed to be handled before they could speak again. Sirus's last words in her mind were: *I'll be seeing you sooner than you may think.*

She didn't mind that. He would either come back a friend or a foe. She'd seen him as a foe before, and she didn't mind history repeating itself. She knew he didn't either. Much like the last night in the rebel Palace, she slept like a stone.

29

LONNIE

HIS HANDS RESTED IN HIS LAP. THE MUSCLES TWITCHED, AND THE shaking could not be controlled. The time of trying to prove things to Teacher Simon had long passed; he was afraid. No matter which way Lonnie chose to mask that fact, the man...or whatever he was...would figuratively and literally see through it.

There was a realization that took place within Lonnie's very soul there in the home of the woman who had lived her entire life for the teacher, who was now driving the white van like nothing meaningful and downright disturbing had happened only moments ago. Not moments, it was hours ago. He'd been in a state of shock and had sat there for hours watching Laila's body slowly stiffen and release its bowels.

They drove on the highway, coming to slow maneuvers whenever they got to a cluster of old immobile vehicles. No doubt they belonged to motorists who had gotten their internal alarm of the sickness en route to some unimportant location. That's how sudden and vicious the pandemic was. Hearing about something and seeing pictures of certain aspects did nothing to prepare you for living in the real world.

The headlights of the van were blindingly bright, and that was a good thing. Without them they would have no idea where they were going, as the evening became pitch dark during the drive. Lonnie didn't notice any of it. He could only see one thing, and that was an old black woman bulldozing through her eyes and any soft tissue on her face. She had dug deeply, like she was trying to find a prize buried deep down in the sand. And the screaming...the screaming never stopped. The sound or octave of the scream stayed exactly the same, from the time her own jaw unhinged to the very last moment that ended with half her face lying on the lap of her dress or on the floor next to the rocking chair.

Murder was a new concept for him, but it came easy. He was exceptional at the act of killing and had been trained to murder without thinking of the victim. It made sense to him; if you were able to reduce the target to no more than a mission's objective, following through with the shot, stab, or final neck snap would be that much easier. But...what Teacher Simon did to Laila was different, and Lonnie's brain would not cease playing it on a loop.

The teacher hadn't spoken a word to him since he got back in the car, and Lonnie was too frozen with fear to even regard him in any way, verbally or visually. One thing did sit in his mind right beneath the vision of the last few hours though, and that was: why? *Why did Lonnie need to come along for the ride to capture Mary? If Teacher Simon was capable of inflicting madness onto a person by simply looking at them... what purpose could Lonnie serve in being here?*

Simon had said for tracking, but all they'd done was use the GPS the entire time. There was a chance that on the ground, tracking could be possible, but he had a strong feeling that was not the case either. *What if he plans to kill me as well...in the same way?* Lonnie slammed his eyes shut. He wanted to look out the window to his left, but for some reason he could not get the muscles in his neck to turn. There was air-conditioning in the van, but even still, he was sweating. The fear was thick, as tangible as the gun in the backseat. Holding on to his AK-47 would help him feel safer.

Who was he fooling though? Even if Teacher Simon laid the thing on Lonnie's lap, his hands and arms would not bend and move correctly to hold it, let alone aim and pull the trigger. Even if he did, would it matter? He'd learned nothing about those who worked for the Order that indicated simple bullets would kill them.

Lonnie wanted to jump out of the car right there on the highway and run off into the woods to die. Anything that would allow him to be out of the presence of the thing next to him. He strained his eyes to move to the right, because something told him the teacher was looking at him. Feeling his fear, feeding on it even—Simon was enjoying it.

There was a time where Lonnie thought he'd earned Teacher Simon's respect, even a bit of fear. The logic of someone from another place in space being afraid of him and his weapon prowess was sheer madness. Lonnie could laugh at the thought until his head exploded, if he wasn't so frightened to simply breathe too loudly. Then came a voice that nearly made him jump through the roof of the van. It was Teacher Simon.

"Are you afraid, young man?"

The van and the world in general became quieter than Lonnie ever remembered in the past. There was nothing but him, the teacher, and the isolation of the question reverberating through the vehicle. Are you afraid? Are you afraid? ARE YOU AFRAID? Lonnie could not answer, nor would he look at Teacher Simon, even if he could convince his body to actually move. He'd never look at him again—as long as he lived, he would not.

The eyes…those were his weapons. That's why when they'd left the Palace and Lonnie asked him why he was not bringing a firearm, the oddly built teacher only smirked and said, "That's what I have you for." Even then, Simon had played his cruel games, knowing what he was and what he could do. Lonnie, all of them…they were nothing more than ants on the ground to the Order.

"Speak to me. If we can't communicate, then that would make clear to me that your uses have come to an end," Teacher Simon said.

Lonnie felt panicked at those words. That was a threat if he'd ever heard one. He wanted to say something back. Getting his vocal cords to do the work was the hard part. His throat felt raw and rusty, but why? *Was I screaming along with the self-mutilating old black woman?*

146

Could that have been true? He barely remembered how his body had reacted to the trauma, but it was most definitely possible. Had Teacher Simon witnessed him screaming? A silly bout of shame came over him.

"What you saw was no big deal. I granted her final wish...the only thing she'd ever wanted in life. The outcome may not have been how she thought it would play out—most things work that way though. Wouldn't you agree?"

He cleared his throat, hurting himself further to get out a word or two. He knew his very life depended on his ability to speak now.

"Y-Yes...yes sir," Lonnie said. The inner workings of his throat were swollen and raw.

"So, you do understand, and you are not afraid, right? We have a job to do, so, I'll ask once more. Are you afraid?"

"No...no sir." Lonnie tasted blood in his mouth with each word he was able to get out. He'd never been so happy to utter five words in his life; those words may have saved him.

"Good, now get some rest. We will take Mary tomorrow. Then this will all come to an end. I'll go back to where I came from, and I'll be sure to let me superiors know how brave you have been." Teacher Simon turned his head to look at Lonnie. Lonnie could see the wide smile on the teacher's face out of his peripheral vision. And it terrified him.

BRANDEN

THE LIGHT BEAMING THROUGH THE SHEER WHITE CURTAINS STIRRED Branden awake. Mary must have woken up before him and opened the darker set of curtains. Branden was not angry though, they needed to get on their way. To where, he was not sure, and he didn't know if Mary had an idea. Maybe they could do a bit more practicing with her power. He thought she was close to understanding the nature of the weapon and herself.

Branden rose to his feet before stretching. Every morning should be started with a deep stretch and a sound back-cracking. Something his father taught him, so he did just that. His mouth tasted horrible; sleeping with old jerky in your teeth was not ideal, but without someone to cook him proper meals, he'd been winging it on the nutrition front. Hunting was an option, but as of late, Branden was more concerned with hunting men more so than small animals.

Looking around the living room of the home, he saw it was not much different than any house he'd lived in before. There were family photos, pictures of amusing quotes, and of course, portraits of Jesus. He could have slept on the couch the night before, but he chose not to because the floor was best for his back. There was something telling him that the day would be special, or maybe just more dangerous than usual.

Branden made his way to the first-floor bathroom after grabbing his backpack, which held a tube of toothpaste and a red toothbrush. The reflection looking back at him in the mirror above the sink transformed more into the face of his father every time they met. He could even see a mustache actually trying to sprout up; his mother would get a kick out of that.

He brushed his teeth with the left-over water they'd gathered from the night before. He then grabbed the worn washcloth from his bag to wash his face. Mary hadn't made a peep and was no longer on the loveseat. Immediately, the thought occurred to him: *What if she left me here? What if she left to go after those Order guys on her own?*

The thought made more and more sense as he stuffed the things back into his bag and swung it over his shoulder. There would be no time to do anything decent with his hair, but before leaving the bathroom, Branden wet both hands by dumping them into the bucket of not so clean water and then pushed all ten fingers through his almond-colored locks. The hair lay back on his head easy enough as he closed the bathroom door on his way out. Branden stumbled over his boots as he rounded the corner back to the living room.

He swiped both boots, sat on the couch, and tied them tightly. If she'd left without him, he needed to catch up to her—and he couldn't do much running with loose boots. The dead family upstairs deserved to be buried, but he would have to be the bad guy on that promise. There were things more important than that, like catching up to Mary and helping her.

Was his desire to be with her so strong because he wanted to be helpful? Or was there more to it than that? He'd asked himself that very question more than once. Since losing both parents, he'd been on an all-danger diet. Part of that was for vengeance, and another part was something else…If he was being honest with himself, he'd become somewhat suicidal.

The world was a terribly lonely place, and there were things worse than death. With Mary, he knew there would be danger, but even more than that, he'd found someone to be with...to talk to, to protect. They hadn't known each other long, but what was long enough to know a person? They both had the same fundamental goal: get rid of those who were responsible for killing the people they loved deeply. That was truly all the knowing he needed. Sure, he could continue hunting men in white vans—but there would always be more and more, no matter how many he killed.

One day, they would eventually catch and murder him; what *could* go wrong eventually would. He had a day of reckoning, like any living entity on the planet. But before he came face to face with that fate, he wanted to make a difference. The easy answer was: Mary made him feel like he'd make a difference if he stuck with her. She must have left in order to protect him, to not involve him further in what had nothing to do with him. She was wrong though; it wasn't her fight alone.

Branden vaulted from the sofa and out the front door, took a right, and galloped along the side of the house. She would have gone that way because it was the way they'd come. Right back into the teeth of those who were searching for her. Well, she wouldn't do it alone. He would catch up to her—he had to.

Branden was so anxious and in his own thoughts, he did not hear it at first. But just as he touched the gate to enter the backyard, there it was again. He stopped moving and just watched. It was beautiful.

There she was, sitting with her legs crossed beneath her in the grass. Her back was to him, her hair so long that it nearly touched the ground. It was possible that she didn't hear him; he doubted that, but she didn't turn to look. She was doing what she did not believe possible only the day before.

Mary sat with both hands out to her sides. In one he could see something balled in her fist. Branden assumed this was the piece of metal. In the other...he couldn't find the words to explain what was there.

The air crackled and thinned around her hand. If he had to try to put what he was observing into words, he'd say that what surrounded her hand and half of her arm was a ripple in time. There were many colors, so many that it was hard to see them all individually. So many that they all became one hue made up of every color that ever existed. But...within the colors, there was a tear that opened and closed continuously.

Standing at least thirty feet from where she sat, he could feel the power exuding from her. It was thick and dangerous, both good and evil. Better yet, what he felt was somewhere in the middle of both. It was a wonder that she could be that close to it without shriveling beneath the power. The weight of what was wrapped around her hand was enough to make him squint and take a few steps back.

He knew why she could do it without shying away—because the power was *her*. She'd figured it out. The corner of his mouth turned up into a smile, and at that very moment, Mary turned her head to see him standing there. She looked back at him with a smile, but there was something sinister in her eyes—something that warned him to keep his distance.

DAVID

"I APPRECIATE YOU GETTING HERE AS SOON AS YOU DID. I'LL BE unplugging from the system for some time. I've gotten word that a certain friend of ours has been tinkering with the reality from the outside. I think you know who I'm speaking of without me having to say." David ran his finger along the lip of his coffee mug while speaking to Teacher Luke, who sat on the opposite side of the desk.

"I've felt certain things as well...disruptions." Teacher Luke grimaced. "If that makes sense? I didn't think too much into it. I get it now."

David picked up the mug of coffee and brought it to his lips. He took in a few gulps before sitting it back down to his right. "Right, so —I'll be trying my best to handle that, but I need someone trust-worthy to handle a small job for me. Simon is out on a separate mission, if not I'd ask him."

Teacher Luke brushed his hair away from his face and crossed one leg over the other. "So that's where he went? He's out there? Nice. I'm sure that's enjoyable for him. Full access to his abilities." The teacher's happiness shone through the biggest smile on his face.

"I'm sure." David pulled the handkerchief from the front pocket of the navy-blue suit jacket he wore. After dabbing the sides of his mouth, he folded the handkerchief and placed it gently next to the mug. "Okay, I'll get right to it. I want you to immediately begin scouting new prospects for Phase 3," David said with a straight face. His words clearly caught Teacher Luke off guard, because the teacher's eyes began creeping around in his head for clarity. Confusion was most definitely afoot.

"Umm...I'm sorry, but I don't understand what you mean by that." Teacher Luke uncrossed his legs, looking both bewildered and interested at the same time. He was apparently excited at the prospect of such a notion.

"You heard me. I need you to find another prospect or multiple possibilities that we could try the new version of Sirus's mutation gene on," David said while tapping on the lip of the black coffee mug. "From what I've read in the case notes, in Sirus's personal notes, there is no reason that the same mutation could not be injected invasively to a suitable candidate. We would then use them to begin Phase 3. I'd like nothing more than to be out of this silly reality and experiment. I'm sure you feel the same way."

"Yes, for sure. I was just not aware that it worked that way. If so, Sirus would not have risked his link to go out himself to retrieve her." Teacher Luke paused, thinking about what he would say next before he spoke. "I apologize for my ignorance, I trust that you understand the specifics on such things much more than myself."

"I do...and my belief is that it's in our best interest to ready someone else for Phase 3 if Simon somehow fails to bring her back in or ends up killing her. You know how he has a propensity for overdoing it with those abilities. He and Sirus are alike in more ways than he likes to admit." David pushed himself away from the desk, stood up, and sat on the edge of it.

"Is there anyone in mind you think may be good to begin trial testing on? You do know the people of this Palace much better than myself; that's why I'll be relying on you for this particular portion of my plan."

Teacher Luke sat back in his seat. He inhaled then exhaled deeply while placing both hands on the sides of his head. His curly black hair bounced around as he sat up again quickly. It appeared something came to mind for him. "I've got it...she has two children here."

David did not show much emotion, but hearing that made him grin. That was the best news he'd heard since hearing that Sirus got himself pushed out of the system.

"Mary's DNA would have to have affected them in some way. They wouldn't be as appropriate for Phase 3 as she is, but they are the best choices we have. Of course, they will need to mature a bit mo—"

David cut him off. "We don't have time for them to mature. Apply physical and mental growth nutrients and begin trial testing on them. I expect this to be started within the next day or so. I'm going to be patching out later tonight. In my stead I'll have you take the reins here. Of course, I'll communicate orders through email. I've already CC'd you on pertinent intel between myself and the leaders back home." David moved from the desk to the massive window behind it. He opened the curtain slowly, allowing the sun to illuminate the office that once belonged to Sirus.

Teacher Luke's face lit up like a shooting star. David could see through the reflection in that window that he liked the idea of having some power, even if it was by proxy. From what he knew of Luke, the man was childish in nature, troublesome even—but loyal. Loyalty would do while he was away. He wanted to check up on Sirus outside of the system and also take a peek into a different program he had a hand in...similar to this one in nature, but far more advanced. That secret program was the reason he wanted so badly to be done with this one.

"Yes sir, I'd be happy to do that for you. I'll have the watchers pull both children from the child center and prepare them for mental evaluations and run vitals. Would early morning do to begin on that?" Teacher Luke said with the excitement of a child on the Old World holiday known as Christmas.

"That will do. If Simon returns with Mary while I'm gone, return the children back to the child center and cease the plan, obviously. If he comes back without her, you will remain in charge. Have him get in contact with myself or one of the others," David said, staring out at the courtyard.

"By the way, those in yellow have gone home as well. They will not be returning, as they have also been repurposed. Sirus brought them into the experiment for his own reasons, of which we do not know. I thought it best they be moved when he became no longer in play. When I leave tonight, you will become the highest ranking Order official on this planet. I believe in you. Take direction and ask questions if you aren't sure. We are not looking for another Sirus, understood?" David placed both hands deep within his pockets, exhaling because he was tired, tired of cleaning up other messes.

"Understood. Thank you for the opportunity." Teacher Luke stood up, pushed his seat back into the desk, and left the office.

3 2

MARY

WITHOUT SOME KIND OF TRANSPORTATION, THERE WAS ONLY ONE THING they could do, and that was to start walking in the direction of Mary's old Palace. It wasn't states away or anything, but walking would most definitely make it one hell of a trek. She and Branden went back into the home they'd stayed at the night before and took what they could use. Then she helped Branden bury the bodies of the dead.

There were five skeletons in the master bedroom up the steps. They were all lying in the same bed when they died. Branden told her that was a common sight inside of every home in the world. The final moments of one's life and how it played out said a lot about the true nature of those from the Old World. It gave her faith in the future, a future she would have a hand in shaping, no matter what it took.

Mary liked the way the white button-down shirt fit her body, so she opted to wear it again after scrubbing her skin clean of the prior day's guilt and grime. The pants were also staying; that was her ode to the late Eagle squad, as she was the last living member to her knowledge. She supposed Marcella or a few others could still be alive if they got away, but she honestly couldn't imagine the Palace-born soldiers not hunting them all down.

She and Branden took off walking in the middle of the street for miles. Walking and talking, sharing things about their individual experiences with each other. His life was like night and day compared to how she was brought up. Hearing about how his parents took care of him, teaching skills and ideas that would be useful to him throughout his life, made her jealous in a way. It made her feel like she'd been grown, not raised.

His story made her feel manufactured, like she was put together on an assembly line. She didn't let him know this; it wasn't his fault, but at the core of her being, it hurt.

Mary explained to Branden that they needed to get back to her old Palace and somehow get inside and into Sirus's office. There was something there she needed to do that would change the situation for everyone in every Palace. She could not say more, because to be honest, she didn't know much more than that.

Just before the conversation with Sirus had ended the night before, he'd told her to just get there, and he'd walk her though the rest. *"If I'm available…"* was the caveat to that. Branden didn't need to know that part though. Trusting him was hard for Mary to do, but she had no other leads outside of firing off colorful beams of hellfire at people and buildings, and that would only get her so far. There were hundreds, maybe thousands of Palaces for all she knew, all over the planet. *"Work smarter, not harder,"* is what Sirus had said.

Worst-case scenario, if things went left…she'd start killing and blowing shit up. That strategy hadn't failed her yet, although Branden's life was to be taken into consideration, as he did not have the abilities that she did. Protecting him would make things harder if they were apprehended, but she was willing to chance it. He was there to stay, and she felt that his attitude balanced hers. He was good for her.

Branden told her that he'd panicked when he woke up and she was gone. He had a bad feeling that she'd left to go on the journey without him. She laughed, and he did as well, but it really made her feel good inside to be cared for. Coming from a background where that wasn't a part of her upbringing, it made her feel a little more human when she could feel that love.

Mary could not tell Branden exactly what she needed to do or accept before she could harness the power of the mysterious weapon. He would not understand, and it would possibly make him even more afraid of her than he already was. He only needed to know that she had taken his advice and focused harder than before. Branden's advice was actually not far from the truth; he did not know that in the darkness of her rage, it was challenging to separate friend from foe.

When he came upon her in the backyard, using the metal object—not even in combat but simply tapping into its power—she thought he noticed something in her eyes. Mary was able to catch herself at that moment and cut the power off, turning off the desire to hurt, to destroy anything around her. The side of her that had tapped into the power of the weapon wanted to use it on him; she could sense the yearning inside to inflict pain. Neither of them spoke of those very intense few moments, probably for the same reasons: it would become a problem in the future, and they both knew it.

During random conversation, they turned a corner onto a street leading to a main road. Branden said the road would lead back to the general area where the rebel Palace was located. Just as they hit the middle of the road, they both saw it at the same time.

Mary grabbed Branden's arm. He seemed to be frozen for a second, but she was quick on her feet, pushing him to the sidewalk and between two houses.

"Didn't you see it?" Mary said.

"Yeah...yeah I did. I don't know why I didn't move my ass sooner. I wasn't sure if I was seeing clearly," Branded said from behind her as she peeked from the side of the house at what was driving slowly down the street.

"That's one of the white vans you told me about, right? With bad people inside looking to find and capture children...right?" Mary said without looking back at him. She kept her eyes on the van while thinking of the best way to attack the vehicle. Using the weapon's power was a possibility, but she thought that might be a bit gaudy for a couple of security agents. *Didn't stop you from using it against the three Palace soldiers,* Sirus spoke to her, and she could hear the smile on his face. *Touché,* she thought. *Touché.*

"Stay here. I'm going to get us a ride." Mary dropped her bag and took off running through the grass and toward the van driving their way.

"But I can help!" Branden called after her.

"Stay!" she yelled at him.

And Branden did just that. She felt his eyes on her, watching her do what she was created to do.

TEACHER SIMON

AFTER DRIVING THROUGH THE NIGHT IN SILENCE, THERE WAS A BINGING sound as the gas light illuminated inside of the white van. They would need to stop and fill up using their supply. They kept a stock of large aluminum drums of gasoline in the back of each of the vans.

Lonnie was still leaning against the passenger side door, shivering like a leaf. It was obvious he was trying to stay as far away from Simon as possible without jumping out of the car—which Simon thought the young boy would do if the doors had not been locked.

It was possible that seeing Laila savagely kill herself had more of an effect on the human than he thought it would have. Lonnie was a long way from the brooding macho man he fancied himself to be inside of the Palace, giving orders and lifting his nose up to everyone because his little girlfriend had been killed. If he loved the girl so much, he should have declined to take her life when directed to do so.

Simon pulled to the side of the road, easing the van to a slow stop. The rough gravel on the sides of the highway made a *thump, thump, thump* sound as he parked. Simon looked at Lonnie, wondering if he would return the eye contact. Of course, he did not. On the outside, Simon's face was emotionless, but inside, he felt pleased at the reaction.

David would likely be angry with him and begin a lecture about sticking to the plan. If Lonnie did not come around, they would have to find a new "hero" figure to couple with Mary when they brought her back. The New World would need both a strong male and female team to direct the others…and Lonnie was not the picture of strength currently.

No, Simon didn't have to kneel down inside Of Laila's home, exposing the full scene of her death to the boy. He thought it was important though. *Important that he respect me for who I am, and not who he assumes I am.* Didn't matter anyway; there were many where he came from and many more in different Palaces all over the world. He could and would be replaced if he could not align his confidence and sense of purpose.

"Stay inside of the car, I'll refill the tank."

"Um…okay. Sure," Lonnie mumbled.

Simon thought the boy was a vegetable, incapable of anything in his current state.

The early morning was bright as the sun just began peeking out from the clouds. The air was crisp, and the sky was a light toasted brown color. Felt like a good day to finish off his time there. The driver's side door swung open as Simon stepped outside of the vehicle, leaving Lonnie inside to hopefully get his shit together.

He made his way to the back of the van, crushing pebbles and ancient shards of broken glass from vehicles and discarded beer bottles littered by madly-in-love drunken couples on road trips. He placed his fingers beneath the latch of the trunk door and lifted it upwards. He stepped back to avoid the end of the trunk clipping his chin. There they were, three kegs of gasoline. Simon grabbed one of the heavy kegs with one hand. Even though he was slender in build, he easily pulled it to the edge of the trunk and lifted it with one arm wrapped around it.

After setting the gas on the ground, Simon closed the trunk, grasped the top of the keg, and lifted the thing a few inches off the ground so that it would not puncture and spill. There was no telling how long it would take to find Mary. He knew she was not far from him, but that could change. There was enough there to drive around for two to three days and then back to the Palace. He didn't intend on wasting any of it.

Simon again set the keg on the ground softly next to the van's gas tank. He opened the gas tank lid, located at the back of the passenger side, and just as he turned to pick up the funnel loosely attached to the metal drum, he heard a car door close. He turned his head to the right in the direction of the sound, and there the little shit was.

Standing there with weak and wobbly legs, aiming the AK-47 from the back seat at Simon. He wanted to laugh, but thought there was a good opportunity for a teaching moment: never pull your gun on someone unless you are going to use it. He wondered if Lonnie had the gall to do it, to kill a teacher from the Palace...simply out of pure fear.

"Well...what are you waiting for?" Simon closed the gas lid on the van, then turned to fully face Lonnie. "You finally moved, and looky there, you got some sunglasses and even a gun."

Lonnie stood there, looking like the scarecrow from an Old World film Simon recalled titled *The Wizard of Oz*—afraid, thin, and unstable. He wore a pair of dark shades he'd retrieved from his bag. The weapon he had in his hand was aimed directly at Simon's head.

"I have to kill you, I'm sorry. I—I can't allow you to live...I don't know what you are, but it's not right." Lonnie sounded as if he were trying to convince himself to do what he already knew needed to be done. "I'll kill you, then I'll go back to the Palace and take out everyone like you." He swallowed deeply. Simon knew that he was holding back vomit.

"Feeling a little sick there?" Simon asked.

"No, get on your knees." Lonnie began circling to his right.

This did make Simon laugh. The idea of a human thinking he could make him bow down. After a brief giggle, he turned with Lonnie to stay lined up with his movements. "Of course I won't. I do not get on my knees for anyone, absolutely not. Do what you intend to do and move on with the rest of your pathetic poorly thought-out plan." Simon stepped back, leaning his upper back against the van.

"I'm not joking. I'm...I'm being serious. Get on—get on your knees!" he screamed at Simon. His voice broke when he said the word *knees*, making him sound like a boy of five years old. Simon now realized that he could not take the kid back to the Palace. He was a threat to the other Palace-born there. He could give them bad ideas.

"Okay...before I do that though, can I tell you one thing?" Simon said in almost a whisper.

Lonnie circled back around to his left. Simon assumed the kid was trying to avoid his gaze.

"Yeah, go ahead. Just don't come at me. I...I'll blow your head all over the van behind you," Lonnie said.

"I know that you will. Just listen. I want you to know that you are wrong about me. Your assumption is that my only weapon is my eyes." He smiled.

"What?" Lonnie took a step toward him.

"You fear my eyes—that's why you are wearing those stupid glasses, right? I can see through those, of course. Besides, like I just told you, these old things," he motioned to his eyes, "they are not my only weapon. Watch this."

Lonnie started to say something. The placement of his lips told Simon that it was likely going to be "get down." He never got the chance though. Right as the first word was about to escape Lonnie's lips, his right eye escaped from his eye socket.

Then, with blinding speed, Simon catapulted himself directly at Lonnie, pushing off the tire of the car with his foot. At that point, Lonnie was a mere seven feet away, and it only took two steps for Simon's legs to make up that distance. It had to be a blur to Lonnie. Actually, Simon knew that was the case now that one of the boy's eyes was hanging from the hole in his face and dangling against his cheek.

Lonnie screamed and whirled around to find Simon, who'd side-stepped behind him and to the area of his left eye. By the time Lonnie saw the blur that was Simon, his other eye had also been pulled from its socket and the gun slapped from his hands.

Lonnie stumbled backwards, screaming and slapping at his face, trying to touch his eyes. It was the same reaction all people had when they were hurt—they grabbed at the area of pain. It must have scared the kid to feel the guts attached to his eyeballs bouncing around his face from his constant jumping and screaming. Simon kicked the gun beneath the van and went back to his previous position, leaning against the van as he watched for a moment.

After the realization of what had just happened to him really kicked in, Lonnie fell to the ground. He got to his knees and, with equal parts shock and panic, he crawled around, feeling the ground. He was looking for something it seemed. *His eyes maybe?* Simon thought that couldn't be—he had to know they were still in their sockets...barely.

"Get up, boy." Simon spoke in a calm voice. He almost couldn't hear himself over Lonnie's screaming and crying. After a few moments, the cries turned into pleas to be killed.

"Please just kill me!" Lonnie begged. "Kill me please! KILL ME!" He got back to his feet and wobbled around the area. With no sense of direction, Lonnie stumbled around with both arms out, trying to touch anything that would allow him to get his balance. Blood poured down his face as if he were taking a shower in it. "Please kill me! I'm sorry...PLEASE!"

"You are only blind, you can hear me!" Simon chuckled, teasing Lonnie cruelly. "You will wander around this dead town aimlessly until you yourself are dead. And you will never see the moon nor the sun another day of your short life. You chose this fate for yourself." Teacher Simon opened the gas lid on the side of the van, then lifted the drum and the funnel to fill the car up. Lonnie took more stumbles, backing away from the direction of Simon's voice.

"Don't worry, I'm done with you. You have no reason to fear me, Lonnie. I'll be on my way now." Simon set the gas keg on the ground; there was still a good amount in it. He walked to the driver side door and grabbed a box of matches from the ashtray. The last driver must have been a smoker. Simon walked back to the side of the van, where Lonnie had fallen back to his knees.

In a low voice, the boy continued to moan, "Please kill me. Please, please, kill me please."

Simon placed the matches on top of the keg of oil. "Lonnie! Stop your crying and decide what happens from here. You have two choices. You can wander around this empty place blind and bleeding out until you die, or you can crawl yourself over here and use the matches I put on top of this keg of gas. By the way, there's still plenty of gas left."

Lonnie screamed as loud as he could, "PLEASE DON'T DO THIS! PLEEEEEASE!"

"I didn't do it, you did. I must be going. Goodbye."

Simon got inside of the van and rolled down the windows so that he could feel the breeze as he drove down the highway to Mary. Also, so that he could hear Lonnie's cries as he drove away.

BRANDEN

IT WAS OVER AS QUICKLY AS IT STARTED. MARY TOOK OFF RUNNING FROM the side of the house where he was, the van driving down the road to her right. She got to the middle of the street, picking up speed as she ran toward the vehicle. Whoever was driving the van had to have seen her by that time. The van began to speed up.

Branden was not sure, but he could not say which of them was moving faster—Mary, or the van coming toward her. He took a few steps to get a better look at what she was doing. It was a fast movement, but he noticed her unbuckle the front pocket of her green pants and grab the metal object hidden there. Just when he thought the van would run her down like a squirrel in the street, Mary sprang into the air at least ten feet.

As she began to come down from her jump and the vehicle passed beneath her, it happened. He saw it...the colorful flame appeared around her hand—the one *not* holding the weapon. Before she came to a landing finish, Mary shot off a maddeningly bright light from her empty hand. The beam of light broke through the glass and butchered the two men in the front seat of the van.

From where he stood, it was clear that the light had sliced the men up, or in half. That was more accurate. The windshield also went as the beam cut through everything in its path, from the back window, through both men, and then out of the windshield.

How was she able to wield the power with such precision? He did not believe the accuracy of the kill was luck. They died exactly the way she wanted them to die. She knew they needed a ride, so she had been careful to not damage the wheels or slice through the top of the van. The front seat exploded in a crimson rush, and there was blood everywhere. The van slowed down, then rolled off the street and into a yard.

Mary landed gracefully on one foot and one bent knee in a kneeling pose. She lifted the arm that was wrapped in the colored fire, staring at it as she began walking toward him and the van of dead Palace security officers. Branden dropped his bag and began running toward her in a burst of excitement and awe.

He wanted to see up close how she'd figured out the power of the weapon, how she'd truly mastered it. In so little time, she'd wielded the power like she'd been using it her entire life. Branden approached with his hands out and a huge smile on his face. He was too far away from her to see the look in her eyes.

The next thing Branden knew, a beam of light with the force of a tornado flashed by his face. The sheer strength of the wind knocked him on his butt before he knew what had even happened. His first thought was that there was someone behind him, maybe another enemy, and she had aimed the light behind him to hit them. When he looked up from the ground, she was walking toward him with her flaming hand pointed. There was no mistaking the devious, sadistic smile on her face. He'd never seen such a look from Mary.

"Mary, it's me! Stop...what are you doing?" Branden put both hands up. He had no idea why, but he couldn't just let her shoot him in the face with a flaming light from the heavens. As if his hands could stop such a thing...

Her expression didn't change. She continued walking toward him as she lifted her hand. He could see now that she changed once her power took over. He screamed to try to get through to her.

"STOP MARY! YOU ARE A GOOD PERSON!" Branden yelled as

loudly as he could. Her hand slowly began to drop, the look on her face shifting slightly to one of confusion. But still, she continued walking toward him.

"Don't do this—don't!" Branden balled up on the ground in a desperate and useless attempt to protect himself. The only thing left to do was to wait for it to happen.

Time was running in slow motion; what had probably taken only a few seconds felt like he was lying there for hours like a beaten dog waiting to be put down. But she didn't put him down...it never happened. The next thing he felt was Mary touching his arm softly. Branden flinched at the contact.

"I'm so sorry...I don't know what happened," Mary said.

Branden peeked through his arms still covering his face, checking to see if she was serious or if it was a trick. She was back; the kindness in her face had returned. The tension in his body released as he got back to his feet.

"I'm sorry, Branden. I can't believe I nearly hurt you. I'll never use that thing around you again. I'm not sure I can control how it makes me see things." Mary had her hands together as if she were praying. A single tear spilled from her eye.

"It's okay...No big deal, Mary. You didn't hurt me, and I know you won't. I trust you," Branden said. Still recovering from his shock, he heard the doubt in his own voice.

"But I don't know if I can con—"

"But I do," he said, confident in his words this time. "You can, and you will. We don't need to talk about this. Look!" he said, pointing at the van. "We got a ride now. Let's go." He walked back to the side of the house and grabbed both their bags. Mary stood there in the street where she'd helped him up, deep in thought. Branden walked right past her. "C'mon, that van won't clean itself. Help me out."

And she did.

35

MARY

THERE WERE NO WORDS THAT COULD FIX WHAT SHE'D DONE. MARY HAD no idea what to say to Branden in order to make things okay between them. He said they should drop it and move on, but that wasn't possible. *I tried to kill him...*Mary wondered why she had missed his head by a few inches. After making an impossible shot through the back of the speeding van, there was no way her aim suddenly became terrible only seconds later.

There could be some part of her still on the surface whenever she went to the dark place, the place that made it possible for her to call on the weapon's power. Something had told her to miss, to not shoot him, even though her physical body had tried to.

Branden drove slowly, messing around with the air-conditioning and pretending to be busy so they wouldn't have to talk about it. Mary knew it was his way to avoid things that made him uncomfortable, but this was not a thing he could just walk away from if he wanted to stick around for the journey. The metal weapon would have to be utilized—it was the only thing she had keeping the ball in their court. If the teachers were anything like Sirus, she would need the weapon again. Even if they weren't, it could be used for some high-level damage. The type of damage that could destroy an entire Palace in minutes.

"What if I can't control that part of the weapon?" Mary said while staring out the window. The wind coming through the broken glass of the windshield hissed and whistled as it cooled her face. The sensation made her feel calm, free in a way. She waited for Branden to answer, but he did not. The knobs on the dashboard were more important than her abilities possibly killing him because she had to become a bloodthirsty death-dealer to use them.

"I know you hear me." Mary looked at him and reached out, touching his knee. "Please...we have to talk about this." She could see in his facial expression that he was giving in. The wind seemed to come out of him as his head sagged a bit. Branden pulled the wheel to the right as they turned onto a street called Fletcher Road, according to the green street sign.

Branden continued messing with the controls on the dashboard, and Mary kept staring at the street sign, thinking of the best way to get him to talk. She supposed they were distracted, and that was why neither of them noticed yet another white van driving toward them just as they sped around the corner. At the last moment, Mary was able to brace her body for the crash, and at the very last moment, she saw a familiar face behind the wheel. Then their vehicle got knocked on its side, and she heard the sound of a million thunder storms, twisting metal, and leaking gasoline.

Branden's side of the van took the hit. He wasn't lucky enough, or unlucky enough, to be born with abilities that gave him superhuman reaction time. He never saw it coming, but she should have.

3 6

TEACHER SIMON

WHILE NOT BEING THE SAFEST WAY TO GET THE DROP ON MARY, THE crash had served a purpose. Especially by hitting them on the side that her friend was on. Maximum damage for the young lad, and minimal damage for Mary, but enough to catch her unaware. His van was crushed as well, but not as badly as theirs. As far as his body, he felt perfectly healthy. Easy like a Sunday morning, as some would say.

Simon walked over to their vehicle, which sat on its roof. Straight away he could see that the boy she was with was dead, or at least close to it. His arm had snapped at an odd angle, and there was a pool of blood on the ground around his head. Broken glass was everywhere, and the car was a smoking mess. No need to bother with him.

Simon thought removing his jacket would be best, just in case Mary was in the mood to engage in a physical competition, as he'd heard she was prone to do. He peeled off his jacket, tossing it to the right. As he moved around the back of the downed van, he had a thought that worried him a bit. *What if Mary died?* David and the others back on Lohar would not be happy about that. Without her, the experiment would come to a halt, and even more resources would need to be applied in order to restart things—possibly from the ground up.

Seeing Sirus again would not be a pleasant situation. The Earth exercise was his baby, the best thing he'd created over his time with the Order. And he would probably be much angrier if he found out who brought the weapons into the program. No way could he find that out though; no need to worry there.

Simon sped up as his anxiety quickened. He hoped he wouldn't find her twisted up like a pretzel with her head in the back seat and her legs poking through the broken glass of the passenger side window. There was a good amount of blood seeping through the windshield and around the boy, and there was a possibility she had died or was seriously injured. Simon was hoping for the seriously injured option.

When he got to the passenger window, he found no sign of Mary. There was nothing but crushed glass and pebbles where she should have been. In his suit pants, black shiny dress shoes, and crisp white button-down shirt, Teacher Simon crouched down to see if maybe she'd slipped to the back.

But she wasn't there. There was nothing at all.

But how could that be? She was riding in the van when he'd slammed into them. He knew that for sure because they had locked eyes just before the moment of impact. Simon stood up and looked to his left at the tall grass on the side of the road, wondering if he would see her there. But again, there was nothing. No body, no blood, nothing...Again, how could that be?

"What are you doing here, Teacher Simon?" Mary said in a relaxed voice.

Ah, there she is. Simon turned to face her. "So, you escaped the van before it flipped?"

"No, I was inside. I maneuvered," Mary said while stretching her shoulders and cracking her neck to the right. "Answer my question. Why are you here? Are they now sending teachers to hunt down Old World members?"

Teacher Simon laughed. "You think I would dirty my hands or leave the Palace for just anyone? No, Mary—only you. I'm here to bring you back. There is much work to do. I'd prefer to go and not fight. I'm not here to hurt you."

"Could have fooled me. You could have killed me in that crash." Mary took a step toward the teacher.

Simon took a step back. "Let's not—really. Your friend there may not even be gone; we can put him in the back and possibly get him some help, but only if we go now. Time is short." Simon looked at the watch on his wrist.

"I'm not going anywhere, and you know I'm not. Which is why you threw your little jacket down. Only way I go back to that Palace with you is as a dead body." Mary smiled. "I'm sure your orders were to bring me back alive, but now that you know that's not possible, let's get on with it. I have to get my friend some help." Mary reached into her pocket then.

Simon watched her, wondering if she'd ever gotten the chance to learn how to use the weapon, or if she was still flying by the seat of her pants. It was small for a Lohar weapon, but he knew that it could still kill. She'd managed to use it to push Sirus out.

"Be careful with a thing like that, Mary. Kids should not play with dangerous things, especially things they do not understand." Simon put out both hands in a non-threatening way. "Just give me the stone. I can even show you how to use it correctly. Though small, something from my star system could be used to level the entire planet…with the right kind of raw focus."

"Stone?" She looked down at the Lohar stone. "I thought it was metal."

"It does look like a dull metal," Simon said. "But it's from my home —quite a different look from the rocks and minerals you'll find here."

Mary shrugged, unimpressed. "I don't know about planet leveling, but I do know it was strong enough to get rid of Sirus. I also know he's not dead, so don't bother telling me that. But Sirus isn't here. That's all I need to know in order to know that I can do the same to you. Sirus was your master. If it hurt him…it may even kill you." Mary's eyes began to blaze, and Simon watched as her pleasant smile morphed into a sinister sneer.

So, she has truly learned the way of the Lohar stone. Didn't think someone as mild as Mary could allow herself to go to such a dark place. "Sirus is not my master. We have always been more like..." Simon thought about it. "Partners of sorts. That partnership has spanned quite some time."

It was clear that she would not come willingly. The Lohar stone and her confidence in using such a thing began to give him cause for concern. Simon took another step back while unbuttoning the top two buttons of his shirt. He knew that force was the only way, as Sirus's DNA saw to it that his eyes would not work on her. *The bastard...*

"That's nice to know. So, like your partner—you shouldn't be hard to take down either." Mary's dark grin widened.

37

MARY

Teacher Simon stood at nearly seven feet tall. His arms were much longer than hers, as were his legs, so striking him was out of the question. That was fine because she planned to use the stone against him anyway. She'd seen nothing to make her think that the beings from Lohar could be hurt by physical damage. Anyone who ever tried to fight Sirus wound up looking stupid; she would not make that same mistake.

Teacher Simon began walking toward her. She expected him to come at her with the speed she'd seen from Sirus. He did not though, possibly because he knew she was capable of the same thing. Mary had the stone in her right hand, which was the hand she usually used to fire off the flame. She wanted to switch hands, but he was quickly closing in. Mary took two steps back, and just as she went to switch hands—he was upon her, next to her even.

Teacher Simon elbowed Mary in the stomach from the right side of her body, causing her to drop the stone onto the grass. The strike didn't hurt badly, but she feared that he would pick up the Lohar weapon and use it against her. They both threw strikes and knees with rapid speed, so much so that they kicked up a dust storm from all the debris. Neither could land a hit on the other, as their speeds were so evenly matched. During the quick skirmish, Mary managed to kick the stone near the car.

With any luck, Simon wouldn't notice and was still focusing on taking her down. Knocking the stone from her hand had to have given him a certain amount of confidence.

Teacher Simon threw a kick suddenly. His leg was so long, the blow knocked her against the back of the white van. She tried to catch herself, but the glass from the broken-out window sliced her finger open. Mary sprung back into action, coming at Teacher Simon with a twelve-punch combo, which he managed to block before he tried kicking her again. This time, Mary caught his leg and drove an elbow down at the base of his knee. He made no cry of pain as the blow caused a cracking sound. He didn't even wince.

Teacher Simon jumped back swiftly on his good leg and crouched down. The leg she'd broken dangled to the side, and he looked like a humongous spider as he placed both palms on the ground.

Mary turned near the truck to see if she could find the stone, knowing it was the only way to truly get rid of him. She was not sure that she could best him in a physical fight, broken leg or not.

Just as she turned to look for the stone, she heard a loud popping sound. Had she not been so close to it, she would have thought it came from the van. But it did not.

She looked at Teacher Simon, who had both of his hands wrapped around the broken leg. It seemed he'd put it back in place. He stood to his full height again and walked toward her slowly. Mary thought he must have been testing his injury before attacking again. She could either try to find the stone or jump at him while he was vulnerable. There was no chance the stone hadn't gone inside of the van, which was flipped on its back.

She would have to continue the attack. She'd never seen Sirus bested in a fight, but that didn't mean it wasn't possible. Nor was Teacher Simon the same as Sirus; they could be different in many ways.

She was in front of him in a flash, connecting punches first to his abdomen. Then, as both of his hands came down to block her, Mary shifted all of her weight on her back foot, vaulted up, and spin-kicked Teacher Simon in the face. There was a terrible crunching sound, and when she made it back to her feet, she saw that his nose lay to the left side of his face. Blood ran down past his lips and chin like Niagara Falls. He never made a move to wipe it away.

Teacher Simon attacked again, but his moves were slowing down. He didn't appear to be hurt, but she could see that the leg and the broken nose were affecting him. It was possible that his mind was cut off from pain, but his body was not immune to injury. For all that Simon, Sirus, and the others were…they were still human-like beings. Or at least, limited by human bodies. Good for her.

Mary rushed him once more. Teacher Simon tried to meet her speed with another kick, which was what gave him the most range. But, he used the leg that had just been broken. *Odd choice*, she thought as she went to evade. *Trying to protect the good leg so that he doesn't lose them both.* Smart, but still an issue for him because the hurt leg no longer had the snap of quickness it had before she'd cracked the bone with her elbow.

Mary slipped past the leg, turning her back and spinning to his right. She got one foot behind his good leg and brought her forearm into his midsection. For the split second it took for him to bend down, bracing himself, Mary stepped back and brought down her foot with as much force as she could onto the shin of his good leg. She let out a primal scream as she stepped into his bone, and her force was so great that it cracked in half.

Mary shuffled back about five steps to observe Teacher Simon's status. The leg she'd just exploded was clearly hanging by nothing more than shredded joints and skin. Still, there was no pain on his face—but there was anger. His eyes were blazing as he breathed hard. They'd been fighting for a few minutes, and he was not accustomed to that. She was, however. Mary had been training with the Eagle squad for months.

She was sure Teacher Simon could not get up and rush her because of his legs. She felt safe enough to run back to the car and look for the stone. She turned and jogged back to where she believed she'd kicked it, just near the front right windshield. She did not see it, and so Mary bent down into the destroyed car to find Branden staring back at her.

He was alive, but very hurt. "Don't try to move, I'm going to help you," she whispered. Seeing his face and the fact that he was alive brought Mary out of her fighting focus. Her eyes began to produce tears. Branden's hand was stretched out to her, his fist balled up. She touched his hand, caressed it slowly and softly. "We are going to get you help, give me one second."

She looked to Teacher Simon to see that he was back on his good leg, doing something that looked like a hop and a scoot toward her. If the situation was not so ugly and intense, she would have laughed at the huge man hopping on one foot in such a dressy outfit. His crushed leg dangled along with him, seeming to blow in the wind.

Mary could feel Branden's hand open inside of hers, and there it was. "I...I...I was holding it...for you." He coughed up a glob of blood, spit, then smiled at her, bloody teeth and all. "Hurry, he's...coming."

Mary cried more and smiled back. "Thank you. He's done now," she said. She stood up with the stone in her left hand. It was time to do work.

Teacher Simon was screaming something at her, and she could barely understand him. The kick to the face must have hurt his mouth as well as broken his nose. *Broken jaw*, she thought. He seemed to be cursing at her and screaming: "THOOK IN MEH EYEEZZ, THOOK IN MEH EYEEZZ!"

She had no idea what that meant, and it didn't matter either way. His time in her world had come to an end. *Her world.* She liked the sound of that.

The kaleidoscope of colors materialized around her right hand. She could feel the heat all over her body. Something inside of her belly burst into flames, and now she wanted blood. She wanted Teacher Simon to be reduced to nothing. He would not get away like Sirus had.

Mary stood there by the van, measuring the hopping teacher as he made little to no ground moving toward her and cursing and ranting about his eyes.

Without much force, Mary flicked her fingers up in his direction. Small beams of light circled his body, attaching to his shirt and pants. It was weird to watch someone burn to death when they couldn't feel the effects of the fire. Teacher Simon stopped hopping and stood there for a minute, looking at his body. The fire burned through his thin white shirt and was working on the pants. He sat down, staring at her. He spoke, the words somehow coming clearly and unbroken now. "I'll see you again. We cannot die...We are all and all is us. Goodbye, Mary."

Mary suddenly realized he'd said the words inside of her mind. She returned a message to him. "And I'll be ready."

Mary shot a larger and more intense beam of fire at the slowly melting man sitting on the ground before her. Burning skin fell from his face, arms, and chest, exposing muscle and bone. Tendons snapped while blood covered his insides...and still, Teacher Simon refrained from screaming or moving. He only sat with a blank stare, burning. There was nothing in those eyes he'd wanted her to look into so badly.

38

BRANDEN

BRANDEN STRETCHED OUT HIS ARM AGAIN SO THAT MARY COULD PULL him free from the van. He was not feeling strong enough to wriggle free on his own. There was also a possibility that his foot was broken, as well as his left arm and maybe his shoulder. Mary pulled, and it hurt, but after a few tries, she was able to get him through the window without further injury outside of cuts from the broken glass. That was fine though—it could have been much worse.

The first thing he noticed once he was outside was the strong smell. He had smelled the man in the dress pants burning from inside the van, but it was overwhelming now. There was a stench that reminded him of ham, cough medicine, and burning wood. He wasn't sure if he'd ever smelled anything like it.

Even though the man was big, tall, and strong, Branden was not surprised to see Mary best him. She was absolutely amazing, and he felt the crush that he'd never been able to admit to himself growing. How could he *not* be attracted to her? She was beautiful and had the strength of a god, if there was such a thing (he thought not). And the best part of it was, she cared about him too. Branden wasn't sure if it was in the little-brother way, or if there was the slightest chance that it was romantic. He wished for the latter, but the truth was, he'd take her in any capacity that she would allow. She'd spoken about the man she'd loved before. The one the Order killed—Jacob, he believed the man's name was.

Branden knew Mary had a deep love for Jacob. And even in their short time together, he already knew her feelings for the man she lost would never go away. *Jacob must have been a great guy*, Branden thought as he got to his feet. He wiped pebbles and glass from his jeans, stood up straight, and stretched his good arm out, inviting Mary in for an embrace. She came inside, burying her face into his chest. The tears on her face had dried by that time, though he could see she was emotional still.

Good thing it wasn't her dark emotions. He noticed that at the end of the fight with the man she called Teacher Simon, she didn't shoot off the beam from her hand with as much ferocity. Not half as much as she'd used on the van earlier. He thought she was trying not to go so deeply into that dark place for fear of killing him as well.

I appreciate it, but that may not do in the battles to come. Branden wondered if that was the case, but there was no reason to bring it up right that moment. Once they switched cars with that burning pile of bones, he would mention it to her.

"You saved us," he said in a low voice close to her ear. She squeezed her arms tighter around his waist. "Ah!" Branden squealed a bit. Mary let go and jumped back.

"Are you okay?" she said.

"Yeah, I'm good. You just got my arm a little bit there." He pointed to his drooping arm and smiled. Mary made a disgusted face and then returned the smile.

"We will figure out a way to get you all fixed up," she said. Mary's smile went away then, and she took a step closer to him. "I'm glad you are okay...I don't want to do this alone."

"I am too. And you won't have to do it alone. It's my honor." Branden did a weird-looking bow, stretching his good arm out like he was a knight in the presence of a princess. Mary's infectious grin came back as she swatted at him.

"Stop it," Mary said, and they both laughed.

"Next stop?" Branden asked, making his way to the back window. He crouched down and grabbed both bags lying there on the ground. They would need those rations and supplies.

"Same plan, same time," Mary said.

"Good. After seeing that guy, I can't image how terrible it must be to live inside those Palaces. Nothing would make me happier than helping you get rid of them all." Mary grabbed both bags from his hand as they walked to Teacher Simon's van, crushed grille and all. She opened the passenger door and flung both bags inside. Then she paused for a moment, looking deep in thought.

"You know what? It was never truly bad inside the Palace. The teachers treated us well, watched out for us, fed us, made sure our mental health was fine. The Greater Understanding stuff I told you about was a big issue obviously, because that guy"—Mary pointed to the pile of smoldering bones—"would kill you after Sirus lied to you about being set free. But, I'm talking about day-to-day life. That part wasn't bad."

Branden didn't speak. He allowed her to get her thoughts out. She didn't like talking about the Palace, but right now, she seemed to need to.

"But...if there is no freedom, then there can never be peace," Mary concluded. And with that, she closed the back door. She helped Branden get into the passenger seat, then walked around to the driver's side. They drove away together.

39

DAVID

To: Luke (Unknown)
From: David (Unknown)
Date: ********
Subject: Green light

I'VE RECEIVED NEWS THAT TEACHER SIMON WAS UNSUCCESSFUL ON HIS mission. There is no longer a need to hold back on the job we spoke about before I left. Mary is highly dangerous, and if I had to guess, I would say she is heading to you or a different Palace in the area. If she happens to show up there, put everything we have into killing her. I repeat: *do not try to take her alive.* She has a Lohar stone and will make quick work of you and anyone else who does not take her seriously. There is another Lohar weapon in the quarters where I stayed; it's in the lockbox in the closet. You will need each teacher's DNA in order to open it. Show them this email if they don't believe you for whatever reason.

I know that preliminary trials have already begun with her children—expedite those if you can. The sooner we get a match for Phase 3, the sooner we can move on from this experiment altogether. At least for a little while. Her children are young, but they should be powerful—strong enough to take multiple doses per day.

Another thing. I know you all have been quiet on her name around Jacob, but be extra careful not to mention her or the fact that she may be coming there. Obviously, you wouldn't mention that to him, but be careful not to speak about it at all around the portion of the infirmary where he is being kept. Past trauma could make him unstable. Before his mind has been completely wiped, you have to be careful about what he is exposed to. I'm sure you know this, but I want to make sure we cover all bases. Jacob is our final playing card.

I'll be in touch soon.

David

40

DAVID

To: NCP Group
From: David (Unknown)
Date: *******
Subject: Experiment 48 – Palace Summaries

THERE HAVE BEEN UNFORESEEN ISSUES WITH PHASE 2 BEING implemented early in some of the Palaces. More were taken over by the specimens than we would have liked. I've attached the current statuses of the Palaces throughout Planet Earth. I'll be returning there soon to get everything under control.

We can all blame Sirus for not taking things seriously and doing what he normally does. He deluded the specimens in order to be seen as a god-like figure to them. He's been doing it from the very beginning. I have evidence to prove that he does not want the exercise to ever end—he will continue to sabotage and restart. He says that he wants the specimens to evolve, but that's not true. He only wanted *one* to evolve, and that was Mary. I'll take care of that issue as well.

The subject named Mary is still on the loose and killing anyone we send after her. I'm going to stop her. It's more difficult than I thought it would be because she has a Lohar weapon, as you know. We are not sure if she has fully mastered the manifestation of her Sirus-given abilities yet. Reports from the battlefield where she managed to push Sirus from the planet says that while in a killing frenzy, she murdered at least fifteen of the people on her side. The stone is not responsible for this—it's in her own nature. Well, the nature provided by Sirus's DNA.

It's a wonder she has not figured that out yet, but she is traveling with someone—so it's safe to say she hasn't. At least not yet. That is good news for us, bad news for anyone close to her.

Regards,
David

348 of 919 Palaces: Offline
0 of 919 Palaces: Online in Phase 1
337 of 919 Palaces: Online in Phase 2
234 of 919 Palaces: Taken over by rebel forces/Old World members

ABOUT THE AUTHOR

A SELF-PROFESSED OUTGOING PESSIMIST, J.M. CLARK is a word enthusi-ast, and an up-and-coming science fiction author in southern Ohio. J.M. studied English literature and writing at Northern Kentucky University. Now, a member of Cincinnati Fantasy-writers and Sci-fi and Fantasy-writers of America, J. M. indulges in his passion for writing and critiquing work in the realm of fantasy fiction. An avid reader, and transitional professional from lyricist to author, J.M. loves interacting with friends and other writers. He continues to deliver hesitantly optimistic advice, and produce work that keeps fans constantly wanting more.

Join the mailing list and receive free giveaways and exclusive content.

Website: http://www.writtenbyjmclark.com

Email: writtenbyjmclark@gmail.com

facebook.com/writtenbyjmclark

twitter.com/jmclark35

instagram.com/writtenbyjmclark

ALSO BY J.M. CLARK

THE ORDER OF CHAOS SERIES

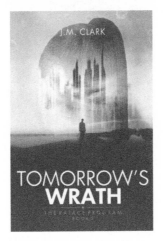

Join the mailing list and receive free giveaways and exclusive content:

Website: http://www.writtenbyjmclark.com

Email: writtenbyjmclark@gmail.com

Made in the USA
Las Vegas, NV
18 March 2022

45902068R00114